THE ROPE

THE ROPE

A FATHERLESS JOURNEY

Steven Wesley Land

WESTBOW
PRESS
A DIVISION OF THOMAS NELSON

ISBN: 978-1-4497-4140-2 (sc)
ISBN: 978-1-4497-4141-9 (e)
ISBN: 978-1-4497-4142-6 (hc)

Library of Congress Control Number: 2012903207

WestBow Press books may be ordered through booksellers or by contacting:

WestBow Press
A Division of Thomas Nelson
1663 Liberty Drive
Bloomington, IN 47403
www.westbowpress.com
1-(866) 928-1240

Because of the dynamic nature of the Internet, any web addresses or links contained in this book may have changed since publication and may no longer be valid. The views expressed in this work are solely those of the author and do not necessarily reflect the views of the publisher, and the publisher hereby disclaims any responsibility for them.

Certain stock imagery © Thinkstock.
Any people depicted in stock imagery provided by Thinkstock are models, and such images are being used for illustrative purposes only.

Printed in the United States of America

WestBow Press rev. date: 3/28/2012

CONTENTS

Chapter 1:   The Secret 1

Chapter 2:   No Miracles 9

Chapter 3:   No Longer Home 15

Chapter 4:   The Scream 23

Chapter 5:   The Pilot 30

Chapter 6:   Storms 37

Chapter 7:   The Skeleton 45

Chapter 8:   The Decision 53

Chapter 9:   Pale White Light 63

Chapter 10: An Angel 70

Chapter 11: Bad Medicine 78

Chapter 12: Spanish Lesson 89

Chapter 13: Black Cloud Day 100

Chapter 14: No Reason Not To 107

Chapter 15: Yellow Shirt 115

Chapter 16: The Murderer 124

Chapter 17: Hands on Fire 130

Chapter 18: Bread in the Desert 136

Chapter 19: Blood Trail 144

Chapter 20: The Calling 155

Chapter 21: Victory 162

For the fatherless

CHAPTER 1

THE SECRET

"THOMAS! REALLY? A wet bed? You're twelve!" Thomas's mother shouted from his room.

"I … uh spilled some water. It was dark last night, and I tripped on my bedpost as I was carrying back my glass. I'm … uh … going to school now."

Thomas sprinted out of the apartment before any more questions exposed his secret and upset his mother. He hadn't spilled any water on his bed. In fact, he hated drinking water; it didn't taste good like soda or Kool-Aid. This made the wet bed harder to explain. Even worse, it was the third night that his bed had been wet when he woke. This mystery could not be easily solved, so Thomas pushed it out of his mind and walked to school.

Along the route to school, Thomas passed an old, abandoned service station guarded by a gray chain-link fence. It sat along the town's main route and used to be popular decades ago. Now all that remained was a hollow plaster building, rusted metal gas pumps, and a partial neon sign reading "kins." The rumor was that the owner's wife had left him many years ago. The owner had never remarried and had no children to take over the station after he died. Thomas felt haunted by the building, as if the building itself wanted him to know more of the story. This frightened him, so he always rushed past the service station and on to school.

Thomas entered the school building. It smelled like wet paint and dirty socks. He hated school. Most of the time he didn't understand the subjects, and even worse, the teachers didn't seem to care. In fact, once, in pre-algebra, Thomas had asked Mr. Modstiff for help with his math work.

"Thomas, I gave the lesson already, and the answers are in the back of the book. Check your own work," Mr. Modstiff had said. Then Mr. Modstiff had raised his coffee to his lips and buried his gray-haired, wrinkled head in a black-and-white newspaper. Now, granted, Thomas knew he could have paid better attention to the lesson, but it seemed like they taught the lessons in a different language.

"If you take the numerator and plug it in to the sumcubchous murinthonarib, you will receive the sum of zuchibob." This was what math sounded like. Thomas knew math was important and necessary for life. Planes flew on math, cars drove on math, and rockets roared into space on math. Like a deaf person who was unable to voice his thoughts, Thomas had a conceptual understanding of math, but he did not understand how to do specific calculations to demonstrate his understanding.

Not all the teachers operated as dryly as Mr. Modstiff. Miss Heirfull taught social studies. She always smelled like something between freshly cut grass and an old sweater stored in mothballs. Thomas thought she looked like the people in the photos police officers would bring in for their "say no to drugs" classes. The policemen would show a photo of a normal, pretty lady the first time she got arrested for drugs. Then they would show a photo of the same lady only three years after her first arrest, and she would look thirty years older. The police did this to demonstrate how fast drugs made a normal person look ugly. Thomas thought Miss Heirfull looked like the last photo.

"How do you feel right now?" she would ask Thomas during class.

"Uh … fine?" Thomas would say.

"Fine? Exactly! And society said the same thing right after World War II." It was here that she arched her back, puffed her chest out like a rooster about to crow, and addressed the rest of the class.

"However, inspired people knew that daily life was phony, and they began uniting to write about the vacuum that sucked the life out of average Americans, who really wanted to break free from the burdensome rules that strapped them down."

Now she would stand stiff, with her arms at her sides, as if Sergeant Pepper were about to inspect her. "Then," she continued, slowly raising hands palms up, "in the 1960s, these brave souls began to speak loudly from the corners of the streets in San Francisco." Her fists now pumped in the air. "They broke free, crushed restraints, and set the world on fire." Here, she turned and made eye contact with Thomas. "Thomas, do you want to be fine, or do you want to be free?"

"I … don't know," Thomas would say, but he really meant that he didn't care.

At least people using vacuums to light San Francisco on fire entertained Thomas more than a math lesson. But still, how did knowing anything about other people's lives have anything to do with Thomas? Social studies also seemed to be in a different language.

Mrs. Duhme taught literature, and Thomas thought she would be exactly what her name sounded like: his doom. It wasn't that she was mean. She seemed honest, and Thomas felt she would not just give him a passing grade like all the other teachers had. Literature class became an escape from his other subjects. Thomas loved stories. The only problem was that Thomas could not read well. When he became stuck on a word or phrase, Thomas's mind kept on developing the story without referring to the actual book. And of course, when test time came, the plots and characters from Thomas's mind weren't on the answer sheets.

One time Thomas made up a report about a book that he had chosen from the class book list. Thomas thought that everybody probably read at his speed, and therefore he did not think Mrs. Duhme could have read every book on the book list. When she asked if anybody else in the class thought *The Adventures of Huckleberry Finn* was a story about a boy and his pet shark, Thomas figured out that she had probably read the book before.

Thomas also liked science class; however, he could never manipulate science like he could the stories in literature class. Science was exact. If you took two chemicals and added them together, the same reaction occurred every time. Mr. Bickerton taught the class, and he explained that science is the process of finding repeatable, provable facts. If it could not be repeated, then it could not be proven, and therefore, it was not a fact. Thomas formed his own theory: that school grinded against his soul and made him more miserable inside. Therefore, it was a fact that school was bad. Nobody ever seemed to believe this theory. Oh well, it was time to eat anyway.

The lunchroom always stank like milk that had been left out for days. The walls were a light-brown caramel color, but they used to be white at one time. It reminded Thomas of the way an apple turns from white to brown after it is cut and left out in the air. Thomas, sitting alone, grabbed his warm, brown lunch sack, reached inside, and … found tuna.

"Hey, Thomas," shouted a voice as Thomas stared at his room temperature tuna. It was Frank. Frank attended the church Thomas occasionally attended with his mother. *Church.* That seemed to be more confusing than math. One moment God loved everyone and everything, and the next moment Thomas felt that his own personal breath fueled the flames of eternal punishment. At least with math the answer was always the same. Every weekend Thomas's mother walked down the church's center aisle, as if she had forgotten the answers she had received the week before. Anyway, Frank and his family always attended that same church. Frank's mom always wore a long dress, and his dad always wore a tie. Thomas saw Frank many times at school, but Frank had rarely given Thomas more than a smile indicating recognition. He was familiar to Thomas—familiar, but not close. Thomas was close to no one.

"My dad took me to the war plane air museum this weekend," Frank said. "We saw these awesome old war planes that were really used in wars. They were old, silver planes with choppy propellers on them, not like jet engines that you see on planes today." Frank made sure to point out the different kinds of planes in case Thomas didn't know. "My dad said he would take me again this weekend, because the museum was so big I didn't get to see it all. He also said I could bring somebody, so my mom said I should ask … I mean, do you want to go with me?"

"I can't," said Thomas as he lowered his head to the table, wondering why Frank seemed so nice to him all of a sudden. Of course Thomas loved planes; he loved everything about them. Planes always traveled someplace different and important, somewhere farther than where a bike or car could take you. "My mom has to work double shifts at the restaurant this weekend, and I have to stay home and watch my sister."

"You have a sister?" asked Frank. "But I thought your dad—"

"Yeah, I do have a sister. Gracie," said Thomas before Frank could finish. "Well … she's my half-sister; she's three."

"Oh, I didn't know. Okay, maybe some other time, then? Well, I can sit here with you, right? That would be nice, right?"

"Sure, if that's what you really want to do," said Thomas suspiciously.

"There were other really cool things," Frank said as he looked at Thomas with the same smile a salesman gives you when he wants to sell you something. "You know, at the museum. They had a display that talked about a bunch of planes that just disappeared off the coast of Florida during training in World War II. Nobody ever found them or knew where they went," Frank said.

"Is that true?" asked Thomas as he turned his head toward Frank.

"It was in the museum; of course it's true," Frank returned.

"Why did you ask me to go to the museum anyway? I mean, you have plenty of friends you normally hang out with," Thomas asked.

"Well, I have always thought you would be an interesting kid to hang out with, and my mom said that maybe if you could hang out with my dad and me that it would be good for you."

"Good for me how?" asked Thomas. He raised his left eyebrow.

"You know, just good for you," said Frank as he pointed one finger toward Thomas, touched him on the shoulder, and smiled.

"Doesn't matter anyway," Thomas mumbled. "See you around."

Thomas tossed his sandwich in the trash and left Frank alone at the lunch table.

Later, at home, Thomas lay sprawled on the floor of the apartment. Thomas's video game box had broken last week, and he was forced to watch television for diversion. His open math book and the television competed for his attention. The fight was not fair. During every commercial, Thomas attempted to look at the math book in the same way one holds his breath before going under water in a swimming pool. Thomas knew he only had a few seconds in which he could stare at the math book before the commercial ended, before had to look at the television again. It was just like having to come up for air.

"How is the number under the line always equal to one hundred when it is never one hundred? That makes no sense. Math is dumb!" Thomas muttered in frustration.

Just then, *Creeeek, thump, thump,* came from just outside the apartment door. This signaled that someone was coming up the apartment stairs. Thomas used this as an alarm system to warn him of his mother's return home in case he was doing something she had told him not to do. Thomas did not like to upset his mother. In this case, the thumping continued on upstairs, meaning it was not his mother, but it drew his attention toward his bedroom, which was next to the front door. He noticed that his mother had placed his mattress on its side to let it dry out. Thomas had hoped his mother had forgotten about the wet mattress—that she would have been too busy, as usual, to remember or to do anything about it. Thomas walked into his room and touched his mattress. It was dry, but as Thomas drifted his hand across the mattress, he felt something else clinging to the mattress—something grainy.

"Sand?" whispered Thomas to himself. "Where did that come from?"

Creek, thump, thump. The stairs echoed again. Thomas ran from his bedroom back toward the television. He did not want his mother to notice him around his mattress, because that would show her that Thomas knew there was a problem, and Thomas did not need to give his mother another problem. The front door opened.

"Thomas, were you just running?" asked his mother, who was walking in the door holding Thomas's sister and her purse in one arm and a bag of groceries in the other.

"Yes," replied Thomas, "In place. I was running in place. A commercial came on TV just now that said kids did not do enough exercise, and they're right. So I just thought I would jog a few laps in place right here in the safety of our apartment." Thomas felt this response was pure genius. He couldn't have his mother dealing with another problem.

"Okay, whatever," sighed his mother. "Just grab this bag of groceries and put them in the kitchen, will ya?"

Thomas grabbed the bag and placed it on the small kitchen counter. The bags clanked as he placed them down. Thomas thought the clanking sounded different than regular groceries. The mustard, ketchup, and soda bottles were made of plastic and did not make the clanking noise. Thomas opened the top of the bag to look inside.

"Thomas," shouted his mother. "Come take your sister to her room so she can get ready for bed. I have to put the groceries away."

"But I can put the groceries away, Ma," argued Thomas.

"Just come and take her, Thomas. You know she's too scared to walk down the hallway alone," his mother argued back in a tone that ended the argument.

"Fine. Come on, Gracie, let's go," Thomas said gently as he held his hand out toward his sister.

They went to her room, and Gracie began changing for bedtime. As Thomas looked around the room for something to occupy himself with, he noticed Gracie's diapers, and he got an idea.

"Let's see if that bed is wet tomorrow," Thomas said to himself with the first bit of confidence he had felt in a long time.

CHAPTER 2

NO MIRACLES

THE NEXT MORNING, Thomas woke up to a beam of sunlight striking him directly in the face. The light squeezed through the cracks in his blinds, peering directly into Thomas's eye sockets.

"Ugh … what time is it?" Thomas muttered as he squinted his eyes to see his clock. It flashed 6:30 in red numbers.

I hate the summer sun, Thomas thought. He liked it much better when the sun took longer to rise in winter. Sure it was colder, but the extra sleep was worth the cold. *Wait a second,* thought Thomas. *Did it work?*

Thomas leaped out of bed and grabbed the legs of his pajamas … they were moist.

"What is this about?" growled Thomas with his teeth gritted tightly. "The bed," he said as he leaped back on top of it, only to feel the thick layer of fluid-filled diapers. They had absorbed all the moisture possible. "I don't understand this," Thomas uttered as he grabbed one of the diapers and threw it across the room.

"No, no, no, no, no!" he groaned under his breath so as not to wake his mother. He kneeled by his bed as if he were going to pray, and he placed his hand in the spot where he removed the diaper he tossed.

"Wait a second," Thomas whispered. The mattress was dry. Thomas was baffled about the moisture on his pajamas and in the diapers, but he did keep the mattress dry: a victory for Thomas in the mysterious battle of the moisture. If he could only eliminate the twenty puffy diapers before his mother could find them. Then she would see the dry mattress, and Thomas would have one less problem to deal with.

Thomas slowly walked to the kitchen, softly grabbed a trash bag, and placed it under his shirt to prevent the crinkling sound from alerting his mother. Thomas could hear the floorboards creaking in the hallway. Someone was moving around. Thomas reverted to walking on his tiptoes to prevent any noise. He came to the edge of the hallway and decided to take a quick peek just like a snapping turtle does when he's looking for food. Just as he popped his head into the hallway … *click, snap* went the bathroom door.

Oh good, thought Thomas. His mother had locked the bathroom door and was inside. On the way to his room, Thomas heard a rattling sound from inside the bathroom, like marbles in a plastic jar. Whatever it was, it meant that Thomas had time to get the puffy diapers out of his room.

Once back in his room, it took Thomas only a minute to place all the diapers in the trash bag. Thomas tied the top of the bag and began to walk out of his room. It wasn't until he was near the front door when…

"Oh no," said Thomas in a muffled voice. "My pajamas. I forgot to take off my wet pajamas and put them in the bag." He knew that even with a dry mattress, wet pajamas would make him just as guilty.

*Whoosh…*down went Thomas's pants, and *whip,* off came his

shirt. He got down on his knees and struggled to undo the knot he tied on the trash bag. He made far too much noise than he desired to, but oh well—saving time was more important now than making noise. The trash chute was just across the hallway from the apartment. All Thomas had to do was simply run across the hallway, dump the bag in the trash chute, and dart right back in before his mother even knew he was gone.

Finally, the knot was untied. Thomas quickly placed his pajamas in the bag and then ... *snap, click*—the bathroom door. *Oh no,* he thought. *She's out.* Thomas stood still waiting, assessing the situation. *Curthump.* His mother's bedroom door shut. Thomas's shoulders dropped. It was clear once again. Thomas walked peacefully to the front door, grabbed the doorknob, and ... *knock, knock.*

"Thomas, are you awake? Can you get the front door please?" his mother shouted from her room.

Against his best judgment, Thomas opened the door and stood there in his underwear, holding a trash bag.

"Ha ha, look at you! You're a bit overdressed for my taste, aren't you, little man? Or should I say little boy?" said Chuck sarcastically. Chuck DiGreecio was Gracie's father.

"Move please, Chuck, I need to take out the trash and have no time for you now!'" squealed Thomas as he squeezed between Chuck and the door jamb.

"Manners, dude!" grumbled Chuck as if he were swallowing something and talking at the same time. "My father would have beaten me silly if I was that rude. He also would have made me wear cleaner underwear, but you know that that doesn't bother me."

"Whatever," mumbled Thomas as he threw the bag down the trash chute and sprinted back into his room. Chuck embarrassed Thomas. Thomas's belly and throat started to feel fuzzy and tight, but Thomas constricted his throat and chest to suffocate the feeling before it reached his eyeballs. No tears today. There was enough moisture for one day, and there were other things to do.

Thomas got ready for school. As he tightened his belt, he felt a prick at his fingertips.

"Ouch," he muttered as he looked at his fingertips. "Splinters? How did I get splinters in my fingers? My bed frame is metal." When Thomas thought about it, there wasn't any wood in the house—at least nothing he remembered touching. And based on how deep these splinters were, he would have remembered touching this wood. He must have been too excited earlier in the morning to have noticed the splinters.

"Thomas, let's go," shouted his mother. "Chuck is taking you to school after he drops Gracie at daycare."

"No thanks," Thomas said sternly as he look directly into Chuck's eyes. "I'll walk."

"Whatever, honey, don't forget your lunch. It's in the brown bag in the kitchen. I made it last night."

Thomas walked to school. He arrived at the school's entrance dazed, not remembering how he got there. He didn't even notice the service station. Thoughts clustered Thomas's mind, not allowing him focus on his surroundings. The moisture, the sand, the splinters—oh yeah, and Chuck. *What a jerk,* Thomas thought. *He has no idea what I'm going through. Now I know why mom calls him a ... thump.*

"What the heck, kid?" shouted Broch Sketchelmanger (known as Sketch). He was one of those linequarters or backfencers: the big guy on the football team who prevents other players from going around him. And big he was. He was fourteen but looked twenty-five. Many times people who didn't know him mistook him for the janitor. "I said what the heck, kid? You just bumped into me. Are you trying to prove you're tough?"

"Look, Sketch," said Thomas, "I didn't see you! I meant nothing by it. Sorry, all right, just leave me alone!"

"Sketch? Do you know me? I sure as heck don't know you!" Sketch yelled loudly.

Nobody knew Thomas, but the whole school noticed him now. A crowd swarmed like bees discovering fresh nectar. Lowly Thomas, who had sat alone and unnoticed at lunch for years, had in a split second found himself the pinnacle of the school's attention. Every action and word in these next few seconds would define Thomas from this moment on in the eyes of his peers. Boys and girls—girls whose cascading, shiny hair and changing bodies Thomas had just began to notice—were watching.

"You know, kid, my dad says there are two different men in this world: meat-eaters and those that bow to the meat-eaters," said Sketch as he approached Thomas with raised, flailing arms.

"You look like you eat too much meat," said Thomas, desperate to sway the conflict in his favor. And it worked; the crowd chuckled in unison. For a moment, Thomas felt elated. A warm feeling traveled throughout his body. Thomas used a skill in his power to briefly improve his quality of life. But that warm feeling turned to ice cold numbness when Thomas saw Sketch's right, clenched fist thrusting toward Thomas's face. Thomas's insult may have gained the crowd's favor, but it enraged Sketch. Thomas's mind, searching for a solution, flashed to the one church service he could remember, *"And whatever you shall ask in my name, you shall receive."*

"God, give me victory," Thomas prayed under his breath as he raised his tight fists out in front of his face.

Thwack.

The next thing Thomas recalled were the white, puffy clouds slowly drifting away in the sky. Numbness covered his face from his left eye socket down to the left side of his lips, but he could feel the blades of grass touching his ears. The pain was not throbbing yet, but a steady, constant pressure made Thomas feel like someone was standing on his face. Metallic-tasting blood covered his tongue and dripped down his throat. But this didn't bother Thomas. What hurt Thomas was that the prayer failed. For a split second, Thomas expected to see one of those miracles, the kind that becomes obvious to the observers that God had acted. Thomas thought maybe he could have thrown Sketch onto the school roof with God-given superpower; now that would be something people could believe in. But not today; there was no miracle.

The rest of the day wasn't important. At home, Thomas lay on his bed staring at the ceiling. His mother was not yet home, but that didn't matter. Nothing mattered anymore. Thomas knew he wasn't popular or cool, nor did he ever want to be, but now he had no hope of even being accepted. Thomas had no hope of anything, especially not of God answering his prayers.

"I doubt anybody will ever help me. I doubt it even matters," Thomas mumbled. Then out of emotional exhaustion, Thomas drifted to sleep.

"Wake up, Thomas!" shouted a man's voice. "It's time to get moving."

"Who is that?" muttered Thomas, still half-asleep. "Chuck? What are you doing in my room again? They told you that you can't …"

"Chuck? Give me more credit than that mistake of your mother's."

Realizing he didn't recognize the voice, Thomas opened his eyes rapidly in order to see who the man in his room really was. Only now that his eyes were opened, Thomas saw that he no longer lay in his room.

CHAPTER 3

NO LONGER HOME

THOMAS QUICKLY SAT up, placing his hands on the ground. "Sand!" said Thomas as he raised a handful of it and then let it gently fall between the cracks in his hand. He sat on a small riverbank. The river, looking like glass, flowed smoothly, not more than ten feet from Thomas. Sheer, red rock bordered the other side of the river, and as Thomas looked behind him, he saw the same smooth, red sheer rock; Thomas was in a canyon.

"Let's move, Thomas," said a man standing at the river's edge. The man appeared to be about thirty. He wore brown, thick pants, a leather jacket, and a brown, old-style round derby hat.

"Let's go where? Where am I? Who are you, and why do you look like Indiana Jones?" questioned Thomas nervously.

"One at a time, kid. First, I don't know exactly where we are going. That will be more up to you than me. This place … this is the Rio Vida. Me, I'm Solomon, but you could call me Sal. Oh yeah, ha, ha … and Indiana Jones? Well, Indi and I were both seekers; but I suppose if he knew the things I know, he never would have wasted his time risking his life looking for mere objects. Now come on, let's go."

"Look, Sal, I don't know how you know me or why you talk to me like I'm supposed to listen to you. But I've never heard of this Rio Verde, and I've never heard of you; why should I trust you?" Thomas said a little less nervously and a little more angrily.

"Thomas, look, it's Rio Vida. Pay attention the first time; that's partially why you're here. Also, the river will soon rise, and this small shore will be under water. It's your choice, but I suggest you hop on this raft and come with me."

Thomas saw the ripples forming in the water and the small wakes splashing against the sheer cliffs and on the shore. The water line had crept up without him noticing, and now the shore line sat a mere five feet from Thomas.

"Let's get the first lesson out of the way," said Sal. "The river always flows forward. You can choose to flow with it, or you can fight against it. It makes no difference to the river."

"That's not fair," grunted Thomas. "I didn't choose to be here, wherever the heck we are. Why should I be forced to have to do anything?"

"Now you're getting it, kid. But quick, hop on before the surge comes and sucks you under," said Sal, standing on the raft with his arm extended toward Thomas.

Thomas now felt the water at his toes. It felt cold. A low-toned grumble came down the canyon, bouncing and echoing off the sheer red rocks. He looked at Sal and at the raft he was standing on. It had raw wooden planks tied together with thick, burly rope. A wood pole stationed itself in the middle of the raft for support. The raft appeared about as unstable as the water it bobbed on. But there was no more time. The water now touched Thomas's ankles and was climbing up his legs to his knees. Thomas began to walk against the current, but the current became like two fists from a strongman grabbing both of Thomas's legs, pulling and tugging. He looked up and saw Sal gripping the rock on the side of the canyon, trying to keep the raft in place for Thomas to get on.

"No more time, Thomas! I can't hold on forever. Give in to the current. Let it bring you to me, and I'll grab you. Make a choice now!" cried Sal.

There was no more choice. The surge increased, raising the water level, and quickened the flow. Thomas gave in to the current. At first he tried to walk, but the current tackled him as if the river were a football player from the other team trying to prevent Thomas from scoring. Thomas headed straight for the raft, face first. He wrestled to get his arms from underneath him and above the water to shield his face from smacking into the raw wooden raft. His right hand touched the raft, but his body started floating out toward the open river.

"Take a hold of me!" yelled Sal.

Thomas fought the oncoming current to get his other arm above water and grab Sal's outstretched arm. He kicked vigorously to stay afloat, but he felt his body going numb with exhaustion. The water no longer felt cold.

"Help me Sal! I'm scar …" Water flushed into Thomas's mouth, preventing any breath, choking him. Soon his whole face submerged, and Thomas began losing consciousness. *This is it. I'm going to die,* Thomas thought. Finally, Sal let go of the canyon wall causing the raft to turn with the current, giving Thomas just enough boost to grip toward the middle of the raft.

"Kick, kid," he yelled. "Kick as hard as you can!"

Thomas kicked even harder, raising his head above the water. He felt the air on his face and thought he felt Sal grabbing his arms. Thomas felt hope, and hope gave him energy. Soon Thomas had his chest pivoted on the raft's edge, and he could feel breath flowing in and out of his lungs. With some more help from Sal, Thomas soon lay on top of the raft, breathing heavily, slowly regaining feeling in his limbs.

"Thank … You … Sal …" said Thomas between gasping breaths.

"Don't thank me yet. We have a long way to go, and you're more stubborn than they told me," Sal said with a smirk on his face.

After a small rest, Thomas regained feeling throughout his body. He noticed his fingers throbbed even after the rest of his body had settled.

"The splinters!" Thomas gasped as he looked at his hand.

"Ya, careful," Sal said. "These rafts bite if you're careless."

"No, you don't understand." Thomas said excitedly. "The wetness, the sand, and the splinters: they must have come from here, from being in this place. Sal, have I been here before?"

"Sounds like you have your own answer," Sal said as he plunged the paddle in the water to maneuver the raft in the flowing river.

Thomas sat silent as Sal guided the raft downriver. He wondered at everything that just happened. One moment he sat in his room feeling sorry for himself, and then, out of nowhere, he swam, fighting for his life in a river in a strange canyon. He tempted himself to believe he had dreamt it all, but he could not escape the overwhelming clarity that told him he was very awake. Thomas noticed that the current slowed and that the river had widened. The canyon walls grew further apart. Thomas saw something ahead in the river.

"Are those rocks, Sal?" Thomas asked.

"People," stated Sal.

"Just floating like that?" Thomas questioned excitedly.

"They have rafts just like you. Just wait, you'll see."

Thomas watched as they caught up to the other rafts. There must have been about twenty of them, only the rafts carried much more than people.

"Floating tree houses; they look like floating tree houses," Thomas stated with a puzzled look on his face.

Thomas remembered the pictures Miss Heirfull had showed him in class—pictures of the "flower children" who built small huts in fields while waiting for rock concerts. The decorated rafts reminded him of the same crude construction and the raw material used to build the huts. They had flimsy plywood walls painted red, blue, green, and purple; a multitude of colors. Some rafts had rugs and tapestries draped over the sides while others had beaded doorways leading to the inner chambers. Every raft looked similar, yet each one differed from the others, just like wildly colored snowflakes.

"I don't understand the rafts, Sal," questioned Thomas. "Who put all that junk on them?"

"I don't think the people would appreciate you calling their homes junk," answered Sal.

"Their homes?" exclaimed Thomas. "You mean everyone on the river actually lives in these flimsy rafts? What about me? Do you mean to tell me that I have to eat, sleep, and well, you know, everything else on this rickety raft? Tell me, Sal, what is this all about? Where are we going? Earlier you said where we go is up to me. What does that mean, and when am I going to get out of the Rio Vida?"

"Thomas, kid, calm down," Sal shouted as he grabbed Thomas's shoulders. "You can ask questions all day long. It doesn't mean you are going to get answers any faster or at all. Look, you're not getting out of the river; the river is your destination. Where you ultimately go is your choice, but you'll better understand that later. These other people have built up their rafts because they have been on the river longer than you. As they travel, they gather what they need to make their journey on the river as comfortable as possible. Those shacks have been built by people who have gone though one of the river's storms without protection. Wisdom told them that more storms lay ahead and they had better use their resources to prepare for what might come later."

"What is coming later?" Thomas questioned.

"More storms," answered Sal. "The storms are a guarantee."

"Look at that raft!" Thomas said as he pointed to a raft that had three stories of a brightly painted gold plywood house on it. On the third level, a big letter B made out of shiny rocks beckoned for attention. "The bottom part of the raft can barely stay above water. What is that person doing?"

"Ask him yourself, Thomas," Sal said. "I'll move the raft a little closer so you can call to him and get his attention."

"I don't know him." Thomas said with a nervous crackle in his voice. "You talk to him, Sal. You're from here. They'll know you."

"Just because I hang around the river doesn't mean everyone on the river likes me. Call out to this person, Thomas. I bet you he won't even see me."

Slam … Thomas's raft ran into the three-story raft.

"Oh, oh … I'm sorry. I didn't mean to do that," Thomas yelled at the three-story-raft as he looked back at Sal with dagger eyes.

Boom, came from inside the three-story-raft.

"Is everyone okay in there?" Thomas called. "Does anybody need help?"

Out popped an older man who looked like Santa Claus, only Santa had lost a little weight and dressed like a fisherman. His sun-bleached white beard hung down to the top of his chest. He wore shorts and a tank top that exposed his sun-bleached body hair, and he wore an old baseball hat on his head.

"Boom!" he shouted.

"I know. I'm sorry," Thomas said with his head down. "I didn't mean for the rafts to collide."

"No. That's my name. I like to have a great time. You never know when we're going to hit that great waterfall. I don't want to miss one moment of a good time here at Rio Vida. I've collected all I can, so 'boom' I say. Let's have fun."

"How long have you been here on the river?" asked Thomas.

"What do you mean how long? I was born here," Boom said.

"Born here?" Thomas repeated. "You mean you didn't come from another place and then find yourself all of a sudden on the river?"

"Hogwash!" Boom exclaimed. "We were all born here on the river. You aren't one of them hocus pocus nuts, are you? You going to tell me of some other place before the Rio and that you're going back there after? Look, kid," Boom kneeled down, grabbing the base of the raft, "feel the underside of the wood. It's saturated with water. The water and the wood are the same, kid. One came from the other. And what's inside of us? Boom! That's right, water. Everything came from the Rio, and everything is going to return there. And that's all. So get what you can from the Rio and build up your raft with everything you can get your hands on, because that's all there is. "

"I'm pretty sure people aren't born here," Thomas said, scratching his forehead. "I distinctly remember my life before the river. Heck, how could I forget? It was only a few hours ago."

"Delusions," said Boom as if he were a doctor giving Thomas a diagnosis. "You only made up those memories because you desire to have an explanation and meaning for your life. You can't prove to me that you actually had a life before this river."

"Well," Thomas began, "do you remember being born here?" he asked, attempting to counter Boom's logic.

"Of course not! Nobody remembers his own birth." Boom laughed at Thomas's poor attempt at an argument.

Thomas made a second attempt. "Well, what about anybody else?"

"What do you mean anybody else?" Boom was confused and a little annoyed that Thomas dared to rebuttal.

"I mean have you ever seen anybody else rise out of the river at birth?"

"Of course it has happened," said Boom as he raised his arms out in front of himself.

"Mr. Boom," said Thomas arrogantly, "I'm not sure how much time you've spent in the sun, but Sal, my partner here, can tell you that there's much more than …"

"Uh, your partner?" Boom interrupted. "I know my eyesight is bad, but kid, you're the only one standing on that raft. Next you're going to tell me all about the rope, that hindering dog leash, aren't you?" Thomas turned his head, knowing Sal stood right behind him, knowing that Sal would end the misunderstanding. But there was no misunderstanding; Thomas stood alone on the raft.

"Boomy, hurry, were waiting," called a woman's voice from the top of Boom's raft.

"Gotta go, kid. Don't believe everything you're told; you'll miss out on a lot of fun. The Rio is one big party if you make it one." Boom then returned inside the raft. "Boom! Here I come."

CHAPTER 4

THE SCREAM

THE HOLLOW LONELINESS of the river haunted Thomas. The day drew to a close, creating a deep red glowing sky that bounced off of the sheer red rocks, illuminating them as if they were on fire. The faint sound of the river sloshing against the rocks produced the sound of small crashing waves, which echoed in the canyon. Thomas could slightly hear muffled voices from those on the other rafts, but none were close enough to talk with. Among many rafters, Thomas was alone. Before this day, Thomas had never been to a river, let alone had to navigate one alone in the dark.

Thomas closed his eyes, hoping he could be taken back to his life before the river, but in the darkness of his closed eyes, he could still hear the river's sounds haunting him. A small tear formed in his eye; there was no longer a reason to hold it back.

"Arrrrrrrahhhhhhhhh!" shouted a shrill voice that reverberated throughout the canyon.

The aggression of the voice sounded like a trapped animal, but the tone sounded human.

Thomas could not see where the voice came from. He could not see anything.

"Arrrrrrrahhhhhhhh!" the voice again echoed in the canyon.

Slosh…slosh. Thomas then heard the sound of someone on a raft paddling behind him. The raft came closer. Thomas put his arms in the water and paddled using his hands. Sal had left him without a paddle. But it was no use—the raft behind him quickly closed the gap.

Slosh…slosh. The raft caught up to Thomas and floated directly next to his raft. Thomas looked straight ahead. Fear had fused his neck, preventing him from turning and looking. *Thump…thump.* Someone leaped onto the rear of Thomas's raft and stood behind him. Thomas stopped paddling.

"J … J … Just leave me alone! I don't know who you are, and I don't want you here!" Thomas shouted as he shook in fear, facing forward.

Thomas felt a hand placed on his back, and his body went numb with fear.

"Easy Thomas," said a soft, masculine voice.

Thomas turned around. "Sal?" shouted Thomas as he stood up into Sal's face. "Where did you go? Why did you leave me alone, you jerk? And who's yelling so loud and scary like that?"

"Kid, you really need to stop with the multiple questions. I didn't leave you alone. I saw an old friend, Clemens, drift by on his raft after you started talking to Mr. Boom. I knew Mr. Boom wasn't very fond of me, so I hopped on my old friend's raft, and I chatted awhile; Clemens is quite familiar with people and rivers. I kept an eye on you the whole while, and when I heard the Stainkins scream, I figured I would come back your way so you would not be too scared."

"Well it's too late I'm frightened of that …"

"Arrraaahhhhhhhh!" the voice screamed again.

"Yes, that," said Thomas, shaking. "What is that?"

"That's the Stainkins scream," Sal said. "Years ago, Mr. Jangk Stainkins was on his own trip down the river. Just like you, he had a hard time understanding why he was brought here; he had much heartbreak in his life before. Stainkins never adjusted and never focused on what he needed to do to make his journey effective. He never got the fact that the river kept moving regardless of how he felt. He tried burning his raft a few years ago, and no one has seen him since."

"Where else could he go?" asked Thomas.

"They say he became disfigured in the fire and doesn't move during the day to hide his scars. At night, he floats up and down the river with his head above water and lands on the occasional sand bank when the river is low. Sometimes he finds indentations in the rocks and stays a few days. Occasionally, he creeps up to other rafts and tries to dismantle what others have built. He gets some relief from his pain by sharing it with others."

"Sal, how could this Stainkins guy go crazy because of his memories when Boom said he was born here and had no memories from before the river?"

"Ah yes, Boom. He came here younger than you. He also had a hard life before, but he took the other direction from Stainkins. He soon saw that he could build his raft how he wanted it and control it how he felt was best. Loving the idea of being in control, Boom neglected the fact that he could not control the river. Soon it became easier for him to believe that he came from the river and was part of it. This made him feel powerful, like he didn't have to answer to anybody."

"So why do you think he doesn't like you?" asked Thomas.

"I don't think—I know he doesn't like me. Nobody who wants to be in control all the time likes me. Look, kid, you've had a rough first day. Get some rest. Tomorrow you need to start building up your raft."

As soon as Thomas lay back on the raft, the blanket of exhaustion covered him as fast as an ocean wave that washes upon children lying in the sand close to the sea. Thomas slept deep. With Sal back, Thomas was immune to Jangk Stainkins's screams.

Splash … Thomas woke to river water in his face. It was sunny again.

"What was that?" Thomas asked Sal in a panic.

"Sorry, kid. The river is getting a little rough. You must have got a splash in—"

"No. Not that. Just before the splash, I heard a woman's voice call my name." Thomas said.

"No one called your name, son, especially not a woman. I would have heard her. I know my women," Sal responded. "Thomas, look—a sandy bank with some wood. Here, you take my paddle and get us over there."

Thomas grabbed the paddle from Sal and attempted to guide the raft to the river bank.

'The raft won't go where I want it to," Thomas said in a panic as he slapped the paddle on the water like a woman trying to kill a rat with a broom.

"Stop!" yelled Sal. "First, you need to take smooth, deep strokes. Put the paddle well into the water, and then follow through with your body. Alternate what side you paddle on so that the raft stays stable and moves in the same direction."

"It's working, Sal. I can do it," Thomas exclaimed.

The raft contacted the sandy bank, bringing the raft to a stop.

"There," Sal said. "Grab that piece of wood so we can attach it to the raft."

"But it's only one piece of wood. What good will that do us?"

"It will do us lots of good once we find some other pieces and put it all together."

"How stupid will that look floating down the river with one side of a shack on the raft? We'll look like idiots, Sal."

"Thomas, you have never had a savings account where you came from, have you?"

"What does money have to do with floating down the river? I never have any money anyway."

"That's no surprise," Sal said under his breath. "Look, put the wood on the raft. Wedge it between the planks with some small shards of rocks. Then grab some spare rope from the raft and anchor it down."

"I still don't see the use of just one plank, Sal. Back where I came from, people didn't live in houses with just one wall."

"You're right," Sal snapped back. "Sometimes in that world, people lived without any walls, and you're going to live the same way here if you don't prop the wood on your raft. Do it, and let's get going." Thomas at first resented a man's voice telling him what to do, but he perceived that the solid voice spoke for his benefit and not merely to establish a stronger will than his own.

"Why are we always in such a hurry around here?"

"Need I remind you of yesterday, or do you like near-death experiences?"

"Fine, I'll get moving."

Thomas grabbed the thin piece of wood and drove it as hard as he could in between the two outermost planks. The piece of wood stood even with Thomas's shoulders, allowing his head to see over the top. He grabbed a few small stones similar to skipping stones and wedged them between the wood and the planks, making the wood stay in place. Next he grabbed some extra rope that was wrapped around the end of the raft and ran it over the top of the wood and then under the raft between the gaps in the planks. The wood stood solid. Although Thomas had first ridiculed the thought of installing just one piece of wood, he now felt proud that he had fastened the wood so firmly to the raft. This was an accomplishment.

"Look, Sal," yelled Thomas proudly as he flexed both of his biceps. "No one's ever going to move this piece wood."

"Careful, kid. Make sure that raft can support your head too," Sal said with a straight face.

"Sal, what are you talking about? Aren't you proud of me? Don't you think I did a good job?" Thomas pleaded, seeking approval.

"Thomas, you did a pretty good partial job. Don't forget, you have a long way to go before you have a complete place to rest. Come on, the water is rising again."

They both hopped on the raft and pushed it away from the disappearing sandy bank, setting them afloat downriver.

"Look, Thomas," said Sal. "There's another beach with some more wood. Let's get it and build some more of the shack."

"I'm too tired, and I'm hungry. Is there anything to eat in this place?" asked Thomas.

"Here," said Sal as he reached into his pocket and then handed Thomas some small red berries.

"What are these?" Thomas asked.

"Just berries that grow on the sandy banks. They will keep you alive, and they don't taste too bad either."

Thomas grabbed a handful from Sal and shoved them into his mouth.

"Look Thomas, I really think we should go get that wood—"

"Yuck," shrieked Thomas as he spat out the munched berries. "These taste horrible, like grass. Don't you have anything here like hot dogs or tacos?"

"You could try to catch a fish and cook it if you want, but I don't think you have the patience for that. You better stick to the berries for now so you don't starve."

"I already feel like I'm starving … Hey, what is that fog way down there? Is that smoke?"

Thomas noticed the white, puffy haze that sat at the end of the canyon. It wafted and pulsated, becoming bigger and then smaller again, like a balloon being inflated and then deflated. The haze seemed alive.

"That, Thomas, is the mist from the waterfall."

"The waterfall?" questioned Thomas excitedly. "Boom talked about the waterfall. He said we never know when we're going to hit it. What does he mean? How do we get around it?"

"We don't get around it. The waterfall is the end of the river."

Thomas stared at Sal for a moment, saying nothing. Thomas's face looked as though Sal had spoken to him in Chinese.

"Where are the million questions I've become so accustomed to?" Sal asked with a look of satisfaction.

"Let me get this right: all we have here is this river. I'm supposed to float on this rickety raft and find wood just as rickety to build a flimsy shack only to have all of this go over a waterfall with me onboard?"

"Yeah, that's about it," Sal responded as if Thomas were double checking a grocery list.

"So, what happens after the waterfall? If everything I do is just going to wash away, why would I want to—"

"Help me! Help me please!" shouted a man's voice from behind Thomas's raft. "He got me, and my raft is breaking apart."

CHAPTER 5

THE PILOT

"I THOUGHT HE sounded close last night," Sal stated.

"Who sounded close?" Thomas asked, confused.

"Stainkins, Thomas. Now throw some spare rope to that guy on the raft."

Thomas heaved the burly rope on his own raft toward the stranded rafter. The man was about twenty-two years old, slender and clean shaven, with short brown hair, and he was wearing a light brown flight suit. His raft had a complete shack on it, with three sides and a top cover.

"Thanks, boy," said the man as he caught the rope and reeled himself toward Thomas's raft. "Here. Hold the rope tight while I wrap it around these two planks that got separated."

The man wound the rope tightly around the two planks that were separated, and then he pulled a knife out of his suit and vigorously cut at the rope, severing it.

"Thanks again, boy. You really helped me out. I was resting a bit when I felt some water on my back. I turned over and noticed that the rope tying my planks together had been cut and that my raft was splitting down the middle. I'm sure it was that joker who was hollering all night long—the one who keeps tweaking everybody's stuff. "

"Jangk Stainkins," shouted Thomas.

"Yeah, that's his name. Speaking of names, mine's Joe," he said as he reached out an open palm toward Thomas.

"I'm Thomas. You're in a uniform. Were you in the army, Joe? Are you like a sergeant or something?"

"Navy actually. See these gold bars right here on the collar? That means I'm an ensign, and I worked darn hard to be one too."

"Is that as good as a sergeant?"

"Sure, boy. After this great war, any man willing to put on the uniform and fight has equal rank to me."

"You mean you just came from the Middle East?"

"The Middle East? I don't know anything about that conflict. I mean the Second World War."

"The Second World War!" Thomas exclaimed in disbelief. "That happened before I was born."

"That figures," Joe said. "This place is so strange. You know, the other day I saw a guy in a smokestack hat, like the one that you see in pictures of President Lincoln. Yeah, he was floating down the river in that hat and a crazy old, thick, black suit. The best explanation I could figure is that this place somewhere between times."

"So there's no time here?"

"No, time still passes here, but it's different and separate from the time where we came from."

"So, you came from a time just after World War Two?"

"Yeah that's right—you know, against Hitler and the Japanese. I trained hoping to get a chance to fight, but the war ended just before I could finish my training. Matter of fact, I was on a training mission right before I wound up here on the Rio Vida."

"What were you doing on your mission right before you came here?" Thomas asked.

"Actually, I was praying, with my eyes open, of course. You see, I was flying a plane. We all were. The training was supposed to be routine. We fly, we drop bombs, and we return. But shortly after takeoff, the flight trainer started to say some funny things. At first, the rest of us just assumed he was joking, but after nearly an hour of him claiming we were on the wrong side of Florida, we started to get worried. He said his compasses were busted but that he knew where we were and that we just needed to keep following him."

"Hey, wait a second. You were one of the planes that kid Frank told me about, the planes in the museum. He said you never made it back."

"Well, I'm here, right? I must have made it somewhere. You're not dead, are you, Thomas?"

"Of course I'm not. I feel fine."

"Well I'm not dead either, unless this is heaven. But really, I'd rather an eternal beach, not a river."

"You said you were praying in the plane. Why?" asked Thomas.

"There was nothing else I could have done."

"Why did you listen to your trainer? If all the rest of you guys knew something better to do, why didn't you just do it?"

"Trust me, I wanted to, and in times past I would have done just that. But really, none of us were exactly sure either. Everyone was confused. And the trainer is the leader, the teacher, the authority."

"But you would really follow a guy, even if it kills you?"

"We don't follow people so they can kill us, but if you're in the service, your job is to follow orders from superiors. And sometimes people die doing just that. Look, Thomas, no one can prevent death. If you spent your time actively preventing death, you would have no life. When it's your time, there is nothing you can do about it."

"How long have you been on the river?" Thomas asked, feeling the subject had gotten too dark.

"It seems to be about three weeks now. Really, I lost count. I spent the first few days being bitter and angry that I was here. Then I got caught in a storm without a shack. That's when I finally realized it was out of my control. I decided to concentrate on the things I could control."

"Do you know about the waterfall?"

"Of course I do. But I'm ready for it," Joe stated confidently.

"How could you be ready for something you know nothing about?" Thomas asked.

"It's like this, Thomas: I saw other rafters with this rope tied around their legs. At first I thought they were nuts. They kept muttering something about the Santa Fe, which runs underneath the river."

"Santa Fe? Like the freight trains that take forever to cross the road?"

"No, it's a large, strong rope."

"A rope? What does a rope have to do with the waterfall?"

"With the waterfall itself, nothing; but it's the best hope of getting beyond the waterfall."

"So you're attached to this rope?" Thomas asked cautiously. "I've looked into the water and didn't see any rope. No one can see anything below this water. How did it get there?" Thomas asked incredulously.

"How did any of this stuff get here? Why were we brought here? I can't answer any of those questions. Can you? But it doesn't change the fact that we are here, right?"

"Of course we're here," said Thomas, rolling his eyes.

"Actually," Joe stated, "I heard a rumor that whoever made this place was killed as he put the rope under the water."

"Killed?" questioned Thomas.

"Ya, I guess the guy hired someone to manufacture the place, but the guy he hired just wanted to watch people go over the falls."

"Why would he want that?" Thomas asked sharply.

"Don't know, but I guess the owner wanted to offer people here a way out, so he strung the rope under the river and died in the process."

"That's so stupid," Thomas exclaimed. "He died putting in a rope no one can see from the surface to save only a few people who will actually try to find it?"

"Look, Thomas, I'm not telling you what to do, I'm just telling you what I've done. You have to attach yourself—if you choose to, of course."

Thomas leaned up against the one side of the shack that he installed and thought about what Joe had said.

"You're a fourth of the way done," Joe said, pointing to Thomas's raft.

"What do you mean? I'm not really good with numbers. I'm bad at math," replied Thomas, ashamed.

"Your shack. Usually most people have three sides and then a cover."

"Okay. What does my shack have to do with math?"

"Look, out of four possible sides of the shack, you have one done; that's one fourth of your total shack."

"That's what one-fourth means? It has never been that clear to me. Hey, Sal …"

Thomas realized that Sal had said nothing during the conversation with Joe, and he felt embarrassed that he had been rude enough not to introduce Joe to Sal.

"Oh. By the way Joe, this here is Sal. He's been helping me—"

"I'm sorry Thomas, who?"

Thomas turned around, fearing what he already knew. Sal had left him again.

"Anyway, Thomas, thanks for your help. I'm going push ahead. Look for me if we ever get back to our place in our world."

Joe paddled on ahead of Thomas. Thomas did not paddle. He sat on the raft feeling like someone poured hot water into his cheeks, feeling angry that Sal had left him again. He felt even worse because for the second time, he had made a fool of himself trying to introduce someone that wasn't there.

"Why, Sal, why do you always leave me?"

"I didn't leave," said Sal, who was sitting on the rear of the raft.

Thomas jumped up, startled, and then whipped around aggressively. "Look, I don't know why you seem to want to make me look stupid all the time. What are you going to say now? That another friend came by again? I saw that no other rafts were floating anywhere near here."

"Slow down, kid. As soon as I heard what happened to good Ensign Joe there, I jumped in the water to check our ropes, to make sure that Jangk Stainkins didn't get at them. I heard everything Joe said while I was in the water. You seemed to be handling the conversation fine, so I didn't feel the need to manifest myself in the matter."

"Whatever," Thomas stated. "This really is all so ridiculous. I doubt if all this is real anymore, or if you're real either. And what's this rope that Joe talked about? How ridiculous is that?" Thomas paused for a moment. "Ya know, now that I think about it, Boom mentioned the rope. He said it was like a dog leash and that it hindered."

"Whether the rope hinders you or helps you depends on what you are trying to accomplish with your trip down the river," Sal stated in a mysterious manner.

"What do you mean?" Thomas asked in the same tone he would have asked Mr. Modstiff to review a math concept.

"I mean the rope itself merely ties you to the Santa Fe, which is the thick rope beneath the Rio Vida. If your goal is to stay attached to the Santa Fe, then the rope is a comfort and a support. But if you don't want to be attached to the Santa Fe, then the rope will hinder you as you jump from raft to raft tangling your rope with other rafts and rocks."

As Thomas contemplated what Sal said, he looked ahead and noticed that the sky had darkened with clouds, the wind had picked up, and the air had cooled.

"What's happening, Sal?" Thomas asked with big eyes.

"Storms!"

CHAPTER 6

STORMS

SLAP, SMACK ... LARGE drops of rain struck the bare skin of Thomas's face and arms, causing the exposed skin to numb. The rest of his clothes became saturated with rainwater. The river roughened, raising and lowering the horizon, making it hard to have any control over the raft. Thomas tried to take the paddle and steer, but the river used the paddle as a toothpick, and Thomas was the food stuck in the river's teeth.

"Lie down toward the back, Thomas, and put the paddle in the water. The raft will be easier to control," shouted Sal.

"B ... b ... but it's so cold. My skin hurts."

"Never mind that. You will hurt worse if the raft slams into the canyon walls."

Thomas laid down with his belly on the raft and his head facing the rear of the raft. He stuck the paddle into the water and steered. He had to look over his shoulder to make sure he was steering in the correct direction. The raindrops fell hard. His clothes now felt like a sheet of ice covering his body, making it hard to move. When the rain hit his face, it felt like fishhooks that tore his flesh with each contact.

Thomas felt like he wanted to give up, but that was not an option. To give up was to die. Never had the need to accomplish a goal been presented so bluntly to Thomas. Usually, if the circumstances become too tough, Thomas could just stop and do something else, like Math class. Thomas would follow the concept until it made no more sense, which usually happened right away. At the point of misunderstanding, Thomas could just give up. Mr. Modstiff never failed Thomas. He just gave him a bad grade, and Thomas would then move on to something else.

None of his teachers ever held Thomas to a set standard. To Thomas this seemed how life was meant to be. It seemed that in the world where Thomas came from, no one held anyone to any standard. School, and work for adults, just seemed like something one had to show up at, and that was the accomplishment. Pain, toil, and anguish were signs that someone was doing something wrong, not as necessary tools to achieve goals. If someone experienced pain while doing something, that person needed to stop and call a professional (or a union representative) who could do the job without any pain.

Thomas then thought of his father. He didn't remember much about him—nothing about his physical appearance except that he had dark hair. The last and only vivid memory Thomas had of his father was when his father left. He remembered his father walking out a front door and that the door shut softly. He didn't remember his mother being in the memory, but he knew that was the last time he saw his father.

Thomas's mother never told him why his father left. However, Thomas pieced together the story from various conversations he had over heard while his mother talked to other people. He heard that his father had been in the army, and he got shipped overseas just after

Thomas was born. His mother received word that Thomas's father was killed in a conflict.

She met Chuck at church a few months after. He had just gotten out of prison and came to church to change his life. His mother felt weak from losing Thomas's father and got involved with Chuck. But a few months later, Thomas's father returned home. He had not been killed but wounded. He was not allowed to communicate with them because his location was classified. He was released by the army and came home to surprise his family—only he found Chuck as part of the family. His father could not handle the hurt and left. Thomas represented the hurt that needed to be forgotten.

Now Thomas thought of Chuck. Chuck seemed to come and go on his own terms. Sometimes he threatened to call the police on Thomas's mother when she did not bring Gracie over on time, like the court paperwork said. Then, at other times, he didn't come to see Gracie for months, and when he did, he mentioned something about getting his state check. Marriage and relationships also seemed like something one could quit when a problem could not be solved.

When Thomas saw movies about wars on TV, he thought that all the suffering and anguish must have been added for a dramatic effect. He believed that no human really had to deal with the pain of having his intestines blown out of his stomach and still living to feel the pain. When Thomas heard of people going through pain for a cause they believed in, he thought that meant when a person feels bad in his mind, like when someone makes fun of another person and makes him feel as if he is not good enough to be alive. That was just mind pain, and everyone feels that. But purposeful, real, physical suffering was not real. Of course, this view began to change when Thomas took the punch from Sketch. And now his very life depended on his own ability to deal with the physical pain of holding the paddle and steering with numb hands and a frozen body during a cold storm.

"Keep it up, Thomas. You're doing fine," said Sal.

Thomas wondered if Sal felt the bite of the cold rain and wind. He took a split second away from looking at the rough river and looked at Sal. He stood straight, erect, and bold. *How can he not feel the sheer freeze of this storm?* Thomas thought.

It reminded him of history class and the pictures shown of George Washington crossing the Delaware River on the boat during the frozen night. Of course, this picture was an impression someone had. Thomas was sure in real life that Washington and his soldiers had huddled much more closely, and that if their faces did look stern and determined, it was because they were frozen solid.

But Sal was not a picture. He was real and right in front of Thomas. Thomas deepened his suspicions about Sal. Of course Sal was cryptic and mysterious, but so were most adults. Sal's mystery reminded Thomas of the suspicion he felt as a child toward the Santa Claus at the mall. Thomas could see the person identified as Santa in front of him; this person was real. However, the inner truth detector inside of us all told Thomas this Santa was an imposter. The man in the suit was named Mike or Sam and was only playing the part of Santa.

When Sal disappeared those previous times, that same inner truth detector told Thomas that Sal had vanished, not just gone out of sight like he said. But who or what was Sal an imposter of? Thomas understood that Christmas was about the birth of Jesus Christ but that Santa Claus came to represent the spirit of giving. When a child asked his parent where the gifts came from on Christmas morning, the parent replied, "From Santa." This was supposed to take the place of the parent saying, "I bought this for you because I love you and want to give you gifts." Thomas didn't like church much, but he liked the idea of Jesus Christ giving eternal life to anyone who would believe. How Santa Claus could represent free gifts more than Jesus always puzzled Thomas, but, nevertheless, Santa represented the idea. He was a symbol. What did Sal represent?

"Focus, Thomas!" shouted Sal. "We are going to hit the side of the cliff!"

Thomas came out of his mental fog and mustered any strength he had left to pivot the paddle and lead the raft away from the cliff. Not only did his frozen body sting with every movement, but now he had even less energy from thinking deeply. Thomas concentrated on holding the paddle in the water at an angle, which caused the raft to veer away from the cliff. Again, Thomas understood that he must hold the paddle in place no matter how much pain throbbed throughout his body. Thomas now realized that most of what he had been taught in life would kill him in this moment. Each person in Thomas's past, whether he or she acted right or wrong, would have to account for his or her own actions. But Thomas understood he could not follow the example of giving up when pain set in.

"No matter what," Thomas muttered out of his blue, shivering lips. "No matter what, I'm not letting go."

"And neither will I," said a voice that Thomas attributed to Sal. Only the voice was far deeper than Sal's; Thomas thought his exhaustion altered Sal's voice.

"That's it, Thomas," said Sal in his normal voice. "We're steering away from the cliff. Looks like the storm will clear up soon. You made it, Thomas, and you had no help from me."

Thomas understood that Sal spoke of Thomas's arrival when he almost got sucked down the river without the raft. Thomas remembered that that time, he had almost gone unconscious as he struggled to get on top, and that later, by some miracle, he found himself on top of the raft; it all seemed a blur. This time, however, Thomas could recall each moment and the pain he felt. He remembered actively resisting the pain and consciously not giving up. This feeling of accomplishment made him feel powerful. The power made him feel warm on the inside.

Eventually, the rain slowed to a light mist, and the wind turned to a gentle breeze. The river stopped its roughness and began smoothing.

"Good job, kid," Sal said as Thomas released his near death grip from the paddle and turned his body over on the raft. Sal looked directly into Thomas's eyes. He smiled at Thomas, but not as before. Before, Sal gave Thomas a smirk like the smirk an older brother would give a younger brother when the older brother was forced to admit some sort of affection for the younger. No. This time Sal Smiled confidently the way a father smiles at a son when the son makes his father proud. At least most young men understood what this smile meant, but Thomas had never received this smile from anyone, and it made him think.

Does Sal know that I have suspicions about him? thought Thomas. *Is that why he's smiling at me? Did I figure something out that I wasn't supposed to and now Sal is mad at me?* Thomas mistook Sal's pride for suspicion.

The river had smoothed completely, hiding any evidence that a storm had taken place. The raft passed downriver at a very comfortable pace, hardly needing any guidance from Thomas. This made Thomas feel awkward because he could not hide behind the need to tend to the raft. Sal had been a comfort to Thomas and still was, but now Thomas had felt that he had tainted their relationship by suspecting Sal was more than he had revealed to Thomas. But at the same time, Thomas also wondered why Sal just stood there during the storm and didn't help guide the raft.

"Thomas, I mean it. You held yourself together very well. You should be proud," Sal said to Thomas. "At the next sandy bank, stop and find yourself some berries and possibly some more wood."

"Yeah, of course," Thomas responded as he looked straight ahead. "Hey Sal," Thomas muttered.

"What is it, Thomas?"

"Nothing," Thomas replied, knowing he was not going to finish his question. He figured that there were too many things about the river he did not understand. He didn't need another problem. Besides, the relationship between him and Sal worked, and quite frankly, it was all Thomas had. He did not want to mess that up with questions.

"You sure?" Sal asked warmly.

"No, it was nothing. Your voice just sounded deeper during the storm. I thought maybe you had caught a cold or something."

"Well, that's thoughtful of you, but I feel fine. Thanks though, Thomas."

Thomas found the next sandy bank and beached the raft. He grabbed some berries that were growing wildly and ate them.

"These taste much better when you're famished," Thomas commented.

"Yeah, things are accepted much better once our need for them is realized."

Thomas knew that Sal said that pointing to some grater meaning. Thomas could no longer hold in his suspicions about Sal. He didn't want to yell and ask questions in a rapid, whiny matter like he had before. He felt that he had gained a new respect with Sal and wanted to maintain that respect.

"Sal," Thomas said with his head looking at the ground.

"Look, Thomas, more wood," Sal said as he pointed toward a sandy bank.

Thomas looked up and saw three pieces of wood that could

complete the shelter on his raft. He realized after what he had just been through that the wood was just like gold to Thomas. He ran over and began fastening the wood planks to the raft. What before seemed like a boring waste of time was now common sense. Thomas forgot about his suspicions of Sal for a moment. He had worked so hard on the shelter that he didn't notice the day darkening.

"Let's put that thing in the water and move. We don't want to be on the beach during the night."

"I'm almost finished, Sal," argued Thomas.

"I'm delighted to see such a work effort in you, but let's move now. You can do the finishing touches to the shelter on the water."

Thomas knew Sal was right, so they both pushed the raft into the water. Thomas used the lingering twilight to do the finishing touches on the shelter. He had fought so hard during the storm and then worked so hard on the shelter that the first moment he sat down on the raft, he fell asleep.

"Take the paddle, Sal," Thomas mumbled as his eyes shut tight.

Thomas could hear the sound of the flowing river less and less as he floated off to sleep.

"Keep fighting dear," said a woman's voice, or at least Thomas thought that's what it was. Thomas reluctantly opened his eyes, saw no woman, and fell back into sleep.

CHAPTER 7

THE SKELETON

THOMAS WOKE UP suddenly a few hours later. The sky was dark, and the river was almost still. The stillness, however, did not bring comfort but emitted an eerie uneasiness. Thomas felt disoriented— the same way one feels after one wakes from a bad dream, unable to distinguish reality from fantasy. Thomas peeked out of the shelter on the raft and saw Sal staring ahead, as if he were keeping watch for something specific. This added to the strangeness of the moment. Thomas recalled all the questions he'd had about Sal's identity and decided in the strangeness of the moment that now was the time to ask questions.

"Sal," said Thomas with a sleep-influenced, groggy voice.

Sal did not answer but stared straight ahead. Thomas felt he should ask again more aggressively.

"Sal!" shouted Thomas with all the sleep gone from his voice.

"Shhhhh," Sal returned as he continued to look straight ahead. "I can smell him."

"Sal, smell who? What are you talking about? Look, I really need to talk to—"

"Behind you," Sal said as he lunged toward a set of hands that had crept up onto the raft unnoticed like a silent spider. Only Sal slipped, falling halfway off of the raft. His head and the left side of his body were underwater.

"Sal no!" shouted Thomas as he ran over to help pull Sal from the river.

"Don't touch him," said a gruff, gurgling voice that seemed to surround Thomas like black smoke from a fire.

Thomas looked ahead of him and saw a white, hairless, fleshy head with no eyebrows and no lips. The skeleton-looking figure climbed all the way onto the raft. It stood about six feet high and was wearing a torn button-up shirt, ripped khaki pants, and no shoes. Thomas could see that the figure had some missing fingers and toes. The figure smelled horrible. The stench traveled through the air up into Thomas' nostrils and into his chest. Thomas could feel the stench in his lungs and tried to push the air out, but every breath out only brought more stench inside, invading his body and suffocating him.

Thomas tried to open his mouth and speak, but fear and disgust would not permit his voice to pass.

"I have been watching you," said the bony figure as he raised his hand, pointing at Thomas with his middle finger because he had no index finger.

"W-w-why," Thomas whispered.

"Because," said the figure "You and I are from the same place, and I hate where I came from. That means I hate everything that comes from where I came from."

"Leave him alone, Stainkins," said Sal, who had pulled his body out of the water.

"You're Jangk Stainkins?" asked Thomas, astonished and frightened.

"In the flesh, or at least what's left of it," Stainkins said through his lipless teeth

"Thomas, don't let him scare you," Sal said.

"I don't want to hear anything out of you," Stainkins said, pointing his few fingers at Sal. "I don't think I can be any worse of an influence than you already are."

"Sal has been a good friend to me," boasted Thomas with confidence.

"Oh really," returned Stainkins. "Look into my eyes, boy."

Thomas, although disgusted and frightened by Stainkins looks, took this as a challenge and with a half-cocked head, he looked into Stainkins' eyes.

"Yup," said Stainkins confidently. "Your eyes give you away. You doubt your friend Sal. And why wouldn't you? With his cryptic half-answers, leading you only to the next step, never giving you anything solid. I bet you still don't know why you're here and probably don't know where you're going. Why don't you know, boy? Think!"

"Thomas, he's only trying to confuse you. Don't listen. He can't hurt your body," Sal advised.

"Yes, I can only hurt his soul, just like you have, Sal, or should I say Solomon the wise? Why don't you tell him about where you came from and why you're here? Public service for womanizing…"

"Look Mr. Stainkins, I'm not sure what you're talking about, but since I've been with Sal, I've learned to take my surroundings and with a little patience and concentration, use them to benefit me. Like this raft. I was able to build this shelter because Sal took the time to tell me what I needed to do."

"Yeah, boy, you built that whole shack yourself. Sal never laid one finger on that thing. I built things myself too. I built a business once, a gas station. I also built a family. But another man, my own brother, took them both from me. I sat in my house praying for help, and then I woke up in this stupid, forsaken place. So go ahead, build, and let this man feed your mind with all this hope of things to come next.

"I'm sure he's told you where you go on this journey is up to you. Sound familiar? I bet he didn't tell you what comes after that waterfall. Of course he didn't, and he won't. So build all your hands will let you and watch it all break apart as you go over the waterfall to who knows where. And then some other person will take all your material for his own use. That's why I burned everything I had. Now no one can take anything of mine ever again."

Thomas no longer felt fear and disgust for Stainkins but pity. "Mr. Stainkins, what about you—you know, your body and soul? I've heard that there is a rope called the Santa Fe that you can tie yourself onto and that it will secure you past the waterfall."

"I'm sick of that cursed rope. I've seen all kinds of fools on this river tie that stupid thing on their ankles thinking that it will magically save them after that waterfall. Now tell me, boy, if nothing now brings any peace to me in this part of life, why would I trust in some stupid rope to bring me anything beyond? The only thing that is real and recurring now is pain and destruction. To expect anything else, now or in the future, makes you an unrealistic fool. You don't wear the rope yourself. Why do you even bring it up?"

"I don't know. I have my doubts about it, I guess, but what if it's true? Don't you want the security of knowing you're, well, taken care of?" asked Thomas.

"Security? You know what, boy? Even if someone came back from over the waterfall (which has never and will never happen) and told me that all was secure if only I fastened myself to the rope, I would refuse to put it on. I would say to whoever designed this stupid river, 'No man can have my possessions, and no rope can save my person.' I would let myself be destroyed just to make the bitter point."

"If you feel so miserable, then whatever, that's how you feel," said Thomas, "but why do you have to go breaking other people's rafts and screaming at night scaring people?"

"Because, it's my duty to spread pain, disaster, and destruction. It's my mission to show all you miserable people that is all you will ultimately feel. I'm the missionary of the ultimate truth of pain and emptiness. And I want my message spread thick with you. Like I said, we come from the same place—the place that I hate," Stainkins said as he closed the distance between Thomas and himself.

Even in the dark of night, Thomas saw Stainkins's gross, disfigured face and body. But as Stainkins crept closer, Thomas could see the flaky separation of the skin cells on Stainkins's face. Thomas thought that his skin looked like white beef jerky; beef jerky with eyes and teeth and a stench that never stopped suffocating Thomas. Although Thomas developed a small sympathy for him, the sight of Stainkins still made Thomas afraid.

"Your overly optimistic friend here is right," said Stainkins, who was now less than two inches from Thomas's face. "I can't harm your body; oh trust me, if the rules of this stupid place allowed me to, I would. But I can bring you fear and doubt, which many times are far more destructive than physical damage."

"Tell him to leave, Thomas," said Sal, who now placed himself behind Thomas with his hand on Thomas's shoulder.

"No one asked you for any more advice, Dr. Jones," Stainkins said sharply to Sal.

"I ... I ... I want you to leave my raft," Thomas was finally able to mutter.

"Fine, boy," said Stainkins as he slowly backed out to the front of the raft. "But remember, I have it out for you. And I will always watch you as I always have. The gas station, the one on the way to school; that's right. I've seen you for quite a while, and knew you would probably end up here one day. And now you have, and you're mine.

Splash … Stainkins jumped back into the night-darkened river.

"Sal, what do I do now?" asked Thomas, still trembling from the adrenaline he used to ask Stainkins to leave.

"There's not much you can do," Sal said, still holding Thomas's shoulder. "The river is still going to move and continue to take you with it. You can choose to let Stainkins scare you as you go, or you can choose to not let the fear of him influence you. Remember, he can't physically hurt you."

"What does that mean? And how did he know about the gas station back home that always freaked me out?" Thomas asked.

"It's just the way it works here. He can't hurt your body. Besides, it really wouldn't matter if he could. I'm sure you're starting to understand that your goals here are not about your physical accomplishments but about how you view things in your mind as well as how those things rest in your soul. That's why Stainkins wants to scare you—to keep your mind on the fear and not on the learning and understanding the process."

"What about the gas station then? How does he know that?"

"Stainkins has been here a long time, and he has learned to get though the cracks. That's the best way I can describe it for now." Sal said this to Thomas with a look that told Thomas no more explanation would be given.

"What about the things he said, Sal? About you not telling me about what comes after the waterfall? The reason that was so scary is because he was right. I have wondered that. I also have wondered why you don't tell me anything more than small one-word answers that never answer my questions. I feel inside my body that Stainkins is a bad man, but I can't resist the things he says because they sound so true."

"Thomas, you have learned much in your few days here, and I have never seen Stainkins be so aggressive with anybody. Don't lose heart now. Understand, I can only guide you along. You have to make all decisions for yourself. I've told you nothing of beyond the waterfall because you wouldn't understand what comes next, and you should not make a decision based on things you don't understand."

"Why don't you just try to explain?" pleaded Thomas. "Maybe I'll be smart enough to understand. I've gotten everything else here so far in this world."

"Thomas, it's not about being smart; it's about level of comprehension. It's the same as if I tried to explain the math behind rocket science to a newborn baby. The baby has no way to even understand the concepts I would tell." Sal paused and looked at Thomas to see if the concept had sunk into his head.

"If you can't explain to me about what is after the waterfall, because I would be influenced by what I don't understand, then why is Stainkins allowed to influence me with things I can understand? Doesn't that seem unfair?"

"It's not unfair, Thomas. The goal is for you to develop an ability to know what is true and what is false. For example, you said that you knew that Stainkins was a bad man. Well, think about it. Can a bad man tell you something that will truly benefit you? Or do you think he has another motive, desire, or plan?"

"This all seems so crazy. I would say it feels like another world, but it already is another world."

"You sure, Thomas?" said Sal with a knowing smile. "I'm sure if you think about it, both worlds are awfully similar."

Thomas had just noticed that the two planks he was standing on were beginning to separate.

"Sal, what's happening?" he shouted. "The raft is breaking apart."

"Stainkins must have torn the ropes as he got back in the river, and now the raft is coming apart in the middle."

"But I thought you said he couldn't hurt me physically."

"You're not hurt physically. He does, however, have the ability to cause destruction around you. Paddle toward the edge of the river before the raft breaks apart. We can't see the banks at night, so we'll have to feel our way along the edges until we come to one. The river is calm now, and being close to the edge won't hurt us."

Thomas and Sal slowly crept along the canyon wall for about ten minutes until the raft finally found a sandy beach, bringing the broken raft to a stop.

"Rest here for tonight, Thomas. I don't think there will be any more surges in the river until after daylight. We can fix the raft in the morning."

Thomas did not argue. He laid his body down on the sand, and when he placed his head down to complete the motion, *bonk,* his head hit a piece of wood.

"Stupid wood," said Thomas. Then he pushed the wood aside and fell asleep.

CHAPTER 8

THE DECISION

THOMAS OPENED HIS eyes at the first sign of sunlight and instinctively went to repair the raft. While he tried to tie the planks together, Thomas noticed that a piece of the plank was missing. Being a new convert to quality, Thomas wanted to replace the missing piece to make sure that the raft had as much integrity as it first did. Thomas remembered the wood that he had hit his head on as he fell asleep the night before. He walked over to where he slept last night to look for the wood, but when he found it, he discovered that it was not just any piece of wood.

"Sal, wake up," said Thomas, staring at the wood plank. But Sal did not wake up; Thomas could still hear him snoring. Without taking his eyes off of the wood plank, Thomas kicked some sand at Sal.

"Cough … cough … what the … Thomas, why did you do that?" Sal said as he slowly got up and walked over to Thomas. "Why on earth would you do something like … oh." Sal then saw the wood plank with the letter B in shiny stones.

"This was Mr. Boom's raft or at least part of it. What happened, Sal?" Thomas asked.

"He's gone over the waterfall."

"Why didn't his whole raft go with him?"

"Because, Thomas, the rafts break apart in the rocks just before the waterfall, and all the wood remains on the river. Only the person goes over the falls."

"How did the wood get back up river?"

"Through the undercurrent."

"It can't be that strong of a current," Thomas said as if he were talking to himself. Thomas's eyes widened as he thought about what he had said. "Sal! That means we're close to the waterfall!"

"Well, yes, but we have always been close," Sal said hesitantly.

"I don't understand, Sal."

"What I mean is that you still have some time. Look, let's use this wood, fix the raft, and move on," Sal said hurriedly.

"But wait. This plank was Boom's. Shouldn't we leave it alone—you know a memorial to him?" Thomas asked confusedly.

"If you want to memorialize Boom, remember the things he said and did and apply them to your own journey if you find any value in them; but the wood he used for his raft has no value or importance to him now."

"I remember Boom talked about the rope. He seemed to think it was a myth and a waste of his time," Thomas recalled. "Does that mean that Boom is gone forever or dead or whatever it means to go beyond the waterfall?"

"Quite honestly, Thomas, it's none of your business."

"Sal!" said Thomas, slightly offended.

"Each man's decisions are just that, his own decisions. No one else can truly know the fate of any other person. What Boom said out loud may not have demonstrated what he felt in his heart; nor does it necessarily indicate what actions he took when no one else was looking. Why do you keep asking so much about the rope? You don't appear to have attached yourself to it."

"I have had many people leave me, but they were still alive after they left. I never saw any of those people have to own up to their decisions. Boom is the first person I knew who has died or gone beyond, whatever, you know. Anyway, I can only picture him now having to answer for what he did in his life, at least his life here on the river. That makes me think about my own life. I want to know what I have to do now to be ready for later. I mean like I remember going over math lessons in school; I thought that because I didn't understand the math that it wasn't important. And it wasn't important when I was eating pizza or watching TV, but then later the test would come. And I felt so stupid because I didn't understand the math and I also felt angry because nobody cared if I understood it or not."

"Thomas, for a boy, you sound very wise," Sal said softly.

"But I get it now. At least I think. I'm going over the waterfall no matter what, and the only hope I have at all of making it past the waterfall is to tie myself to the rope. What did you call it earlier, Sal?"

"The rope under the river is called the Santa Fe, Thomas."

"Yes, the Santa Fe is the answer to my math problem of being on this river, the Rio Vida."

"How does it help you, Thomas, if it is under the river and you are above it?" Sal asked with a curious smirk on his face.

"Well, I guess I have to get a hold of it and attach myself. Right, Sal?"

"Exactly," said Sal with a beaming smile. "So let's fix the raft and get it on the river so you can take care of business."

Thomas took Boom's plank, removed the shiny rocks, and placed them in the sand in the same B formation. Thomas felt he owed Boom some recognition for his life. He thought that the river would eventually wash the rocks out of formation and return the rocks to the river bottom. At least that would be the river's doing, Thomas figured. He then took the plank, and using a jagged rock, cut the plank to fit in the raft's shape. Next he used some rope to tie the new piece with the planks on the raft. He pulled hard, making the bond tight.

"The river is picking up current, Thomas. Let's finish and move on."

Thomas saw the river ripples and the creeping waterline indicating the river was rising. Having learned his lesson earlier about the rising river, Thomas pushed the raft in the water, and he and Sal hopped on. The raft quickly got caught in the current, picking up speed, sending it to the middle of the river.

"Okay, I guess I just wait until the right time and then I go attach myself."

"What do you mean the right time?" Sal asked.

"The rope, Sal. I just wait for the safest time to attach myself to it, right? There has got to be a time when the rope is closer to the top so that it is easier to get, right?" Thomas looked at Sal for affirmation.

"Thomas, you've seen how unpredictable the river can be. There is no time that is better or worse or safer than any other time. The rope is always in the same place under the water. Everyone has to travel the same depth."

Thomas sat on the front edge of the raft looking down at the water and pondering what Sal had just said. What had seemed like the best decision a few minutes ago became infected with doubt and fear. The water, although blue and peaceful, did not allow Thomas to see anything below it. *What if the Santa Fe is not really there? What if I get caught in an undercurrent and can't find the top of the river again?* While asking himself these questions, Thomas began to feel hot in his skin, and it became uncomfortable to sit. Thomas stood up and looked for a place to walk on the raft, but no space was available.

"Aghhhh," Thomas grunted with closed teeth.

"What's the matter, Thomas?" Sal asked curiously.

"I don't know. Don't ask me that … I don't know," Thomas said sharply.

Sal closed his eyes and shook his head from side to side as he turned his back to Thomas. Thomas could see that the doubt in his mind affected his actions and that those actions now affected Sal. Thomas remembered how peaceful and energetic he had felt a few moments ago when he made his decision to find the rope. In only a few seconds his doubt and fear had conquered not only his mind but also his body and soul.

"You have doubts, don't you, Thomas?" Sal asked with his back turned to Thomas.

Thomas heard Sal's words, and he felt comfort in them, knowing that Sal must have understood what Thomas felt. In his mind, Thomas wanted to say thanks to Sal. It was a comfort to know that he understood.

"Maybe," came out of Thomas's mouth sharply. But that was not what he wanted to say. Although Thomas's mind knew what to say, there was a disconnect between Thomas's mind and his body.

"Every question you have probably has validity, having a little bit of truth in it," said Sal softly. "But once you take the small truths and allow them to spread beyond their context, the truths become more of a trap, like a spiderweb, rather than a foundation to build thoughts upon. Truth in its right place always brings comfort. It's out of place truth that causes frustration and fear."

Thomas knew Sal was right. Thomas felt it was better to not speak until the hotness in his skin and body cooled down.

"I have nothing to lose, do I, Sal?" asked Thomas in voice indicating he had calmed down.

"Even if you did, wouldn't it still be worth it?" Sal asked.

"I guess you're right," said Thomas. "Nothing else offers any hope." Thomas regained the excitement he had before. "So what do I do first, Sal?"

"Take some spare rope off of the raft and tie it around your ankle. Make sure you leave enough length to return to the surface once you have tied yourself to the Santa Fe."

Thomas did just what Sal had told him, and now he stood at the edge of the raft. Before he could think up more doubt, he lifted his right foot, placed it over the water and leaned forward to plunge in.

"No you will not!" screamed a familiar shrill voice.

Thomas felt a hand grab his ankle, causing him to fall into the water. But he could not swim away because the hand gripped his ankle.

"I told you I would be paying a lot of attention to you," said the voice.

Thomas turned over in the water, raising his face above the river. Now he could see who grabbed his ankle.

"Stainkins," shouted Thomas as he saw the skeletal villain who held onto the raft with one hand and Thomas's ankle in the other. "What are you doing? What does this have to do with you?"

"Everything. I told you we come from the same place, and I hate that. Besides, I'm really doing you a favor. You think that stupid rope is going to do any thing for you? Even if you do find something underneath the water, it'll do you no good! Do it! Then you will surface only to be the same person you already are. You will still get hot, cold, angry, wet, sad, hungry … nothing will change, and you will waste your time, life, and honor."

Thomas found himself treading the water with his two arms to keep his face above the river. He could feel himself getting tired and knew he only had a short time before he would get exhausted and sink. What made Thomas even more tired was the haunting reality of what Stainkins said.

"Sal, help … me … please! You said … he couldn't … hurt me … physically!" Thomas shouted between breaths. But Thomas could not see Sal on the raft.

Thomas's courage started to fail. But Thomas recalled all he had learned about not giving up and working through pain to meet goals. Even in his desperate situation, the thought of getting attached to the Santa Fe comforted Thomas. He then took his one free foot, cocked it back, and struck Stainkins in the skull. Thomas thought at first that he had broken his own foot, but then he felt Stainkins let go. As Thomas swam back, he saw that Stainkins had a crack on the exposed piece of his skull above the eye. Stainkins began to slowly sink.

Thomas felt the victory of freedom, and to demonstrate his freedom, Thomas submerged himself into the water. He swam downward, reaching for the Santa Fe, not knowing how much time was actually passing. Every second felt like a minute, and still no Santa Fe. The air in Thomas's lungs began to feel heavy and burdensome, and the water gripped his face more tightly, like someone strapping duct tape over his mouth and nostrils.

The fear that the Santa Fe was a big joke started to seem real, and Thomas wondered if he really wanted to die for being a fool. He extended his arms laterally at his side, intending to appear dead as he floated up to the surface so Stainkins would leave him alone. But as he reached out to his arms' full extent, his hand brushed against what felt like a cable that would hold up the Golden Gate Bridge. *This must be it*, Thomas thought. With what little breath he had left, he quickly tied his rope to the big cable, which Thomas knew must have been the Santa Fe, and swam up to the surface. Thomas then broke the surface of the water, rising up as a new man.

As the beads of water ran down his face, he scanned the river's surface for Stainkins and saw nothing. Thomas then looked at the raft, and not seeing Stainkins there either, he began to swim toward it. He climbed on top of the raft, hoping he would see Sal so he could tell him all about the experience with the Santa Fe, but Sal was absent again. The deep inner truth detector inside Thomas told him he would see Sal no more.

Thomas did, however, see Stainkins's body floating facedown. At first Thomas thought that Stainkins deserved to die facedown in a lonely, cold place. But Thomas remembered the sympathy he felt for Stainkins when he heard about how he lost his family and his business because of his brother's betrayal. Thomas remembered how it felt to have people abandon him and how much he desired someone to come along and show him some sympathy and direction. He knew now that it would be inconsistent to feel so much peace because of the Santa Fe and to abandon others who still needed it. He paddled the raft over to Stainkins's body and used all his remaining strength to pull Stainkins on board. Barely breathing, Stainkins still disgusted Thomas with his burned, mangled appearance, but Thomas knew now that he wasn't trying to save Stainkins's body.

Thomas paddled the raft until he found the next sandy bank. He beached the raft and unloaded Stainkins's body. Thomas stared at the half man, half skeleton for a small while and then turned around to walk away.

"Why did you … *cough* … *cough* … rescue me?" Stainkins mumbled, regaining consciousness.

"Because you were right," Thomas said, slowly turning back around. "I tied myself to the rope, and I do still feel cold, angry, wet, sad, and hungry; but now I also have hope, and nothing can ever take that away. Good luck to you, Mr. Stainkins. I pray to God that one day you will have hope too. The work has already been done; all you need to do is believe it's there."

Jangk Stainkins had no reply.

Thomas pushed the raft back into the water and began drifting down the Rio Vida, this time without Sal. The mist from the waterfall began to thicken and wrap itself around Thomas and the raft. The waterfall's roar grew louder and fuller. Thomas knew it soon would be time to go over the falls, and now nothing could be done but wait for it to happen.

Thomas reflected on the journey thus far, and on Sal. "He was the first man that ever took the time to teach me anything."

As strange as it seemed, Thomas knew Sal still remained close. It was just a feeling, not actual communication, that takes place between two beings. But yet, it was more than a feeling; it was a piece of knowledge far more solid than a feeling.

Creak … crack … rumble … rumble. The raft shook under Thomas's feet, and the planks slowly separated below him. It was happening. The raft began breaking apart. The shack Thomas had spent so much time building shook back and forth. The mist had thickened so heavily that Thomas could no longer see the raft, the shack, or his feet.

"Okay, here it comes. I knew this was coming," Thomas said to himself reassuringly. He reached down and grabbed the rope on his ankle, gripping it tightly. "You are all I have now, rope," said Thomas out loud, but he could not hear himself speak. The roar of the falls conquered the air, not allowing any other noise to be heard. Thomas then felt the rope on his ankle tighten. It got tighter, tighter, and *splash*—Thomas's raft broke apart, and he sunk into the water. He felt the rush of the water thrust him forward as if he were a baseball in a pitcher's hand about to be released. All of a sudden, the water dropped out underneath him. Thomas fell with the water for a few feet, and then the rope tightened at his ankle, nearly cutting off the circulation in his leg. He hung suspended for a few seconds, and then the blood rushed to Thomas's head, and he began to black out. But as his vision began to collapse, he heard a woman's voice …

"I knew you'd make it here!"

CHAPTER 9

PALE WHITE LIGHT

THOMAS OPENED HIS eyes slowly. Sensing the great amounts of light, Thomas limited his eyes to a small slit, just like a bouncer at a speakeasy opens the small slat on the door to prevent anyone unwanted from entering. After his eyes focused, he could see that he lay in bed surrounded by stale white walls in a room bathed in bright florescent lights. The chrome rails on the bed enhanced the florescent light from above, beaming it directly into Thomas's face, making it difficult to keep his eyes open. Before he shut his eyes again, he could see coming out of his wrists wires and tubes, which traveled from his body like different roads diverging from the interstate.

"Honey, we're right here," said a woman's voice.

"Mom?" asked Thomas cautiously. "Is that you?"

"Yes, honey. Were so glad to have you back," she said as she lowered her head and arms to embrace Thomas. Thomas opened his eyes enough to see his mother. She was not wearing her restaurant uniform, but her hair was greasy and straggly, as if she had been working extra-long shifts. She had dark circles under her eyes, and her hands shook. Inside her shaking fist she clinched a paper that read "*police report.*"

"So you know I was gone?" Thomas asked, feeling confused. "How did I get back here?"

"Well, you were out for a week," said his mother, puzzled. "What do mean gone, honey?"

"The river. I went to the Rio Vida, and I met a man named Sal who guided me along. And then I meet a bunch of other people—they were on rafts just like me. There was a scary man named Jangk Stainkins who tried to hurt me, but I found the Santa Fe anyway, which was under the river, and I tied myself onto it with rope and that's what saved me. And now I'm here again. You see, Mom, this is why the mattress kept getting wet. I must have been going back and forth to the river; and the sand that also came from the river, and the splinters too, those came from the raft. I had to grip it so tightly at times that I got splinters in my hands. But the best part is when I found the Santa Fe. It was there, it was really there. Even though I doubted … Mom, why are you looking at me like that?"

"Maybe I can explain," said the man in the long white coat who stood next to Thomas's mother. "Thomas, I'm Doctor Skeptigo. I've been monitoring you for this past week."

"I still don't understand," said Thomas. "Why am I in a hospital?"

"Well, a number of reasons," said the doctor, "the first of which is you had some head trauma that caused your brain to swell."

"How did that happen?" Thomas asked.

"Honey, you had a fight at school," Thomas's mother interjected.

"But I went the rest of the day at school and had no problem," Thomas countered.

"Oftentimes," began the doctor. "A head injury will take a few hours to develop any signs. You apparently went home and slept, which is the worst thing to do when you have a head injury."

"But I was on a river. I know it really happened!" exclaimed Thomas.

"That brings me to my point," the doctor continued. "Comas from head injuries often produce wild dreams or fantasies, if you will."

"This was no fantasy," Thomas argued. "There was a man named Sal (which was short for Solomon), who helped me through the river. He made references to my world back home. You see, he knew I came from somewhere else, and he tried to help me. I know it!"

"Oh, Solomon," said the doctor. "I have Solomon right here." The doctor pointed to the metal machine attached to Thomas. The machine's monitor flashed multiple numbers and graphs, and on top written in white was the word, "Solomon."

Thomas stared at the word silently, having no explanation for the coincidence.

"We named the machine Solomon because he is very wise. He monitors your heartbeat, and if the rhythm is off, or if your heart stops, he provides the electric pulse to get it going again. The pulse he puts out is like a suggestion he gives to your heart. Your heart has to work on its own even after the suggestion or impulse. You must have heard us refer to the machine while you were out and placed it in your dream. It's common for people in comas to hear the speech of those near by."

"I know it was more than a dream," Thomas muttered, realizing his story would not be believed by adults and doctors. "But Mom, what about the wet mattress and the sand? You had to have felt the sand on the mattress when you flipped it over. And look!" Thomas said as he looked at his fingers. "The splinters were here. I can see the sores on my fingers where the splinters were."

Thomas's mother looked uncomfortably at Thomas and then at the doctor. She tightened her grip on the paper that said police report. "Can I tell him everything, Doctor?" she asked in a helpless voice.

"Thomas," said the doctor, taking over for his mother. "The splinters came from under your bed."

"What do you mean? You don't know. You have never been to my room. Besides, my bed frame is metal. You can't get splinters from metal."

"You are correct, Thomas, you can't get splinters from metal; and you are correct in saying I have never been to your room. But from what I understand, the slats that go between the metal rails on your bed are wood. They hold the mattress up."

"How do you know these things about my room?" Thomas asked defiantly.

The doctor lowered a picture down to Thomas's face.

"That's my room, and that's my bed flipped on its side. I don't understand. Who took these photos?" Thomas asked with look of grief.

"Look, Thomas, you can see the wooden slats underneath, right?"

"Yes, I can see them," Thomas confirmed. "But who took the photos?"

"Look at those indentations. See how they are the same size as you finger."

"I do," confirmed Thomas again. "But who took the photos?"

"They look like you dug you fingers in the wood and then dragged them as if you were hanging on your bed for dear life. This is where your splinters came from. And the photos … they are police photos, but don't worry about that. We'll explain that later."

Confronted with strong evidence, Thomas sat silent for a moment. "What about the sand?"

"Honey," Thomas's mother broke in. "Do you remember when you were little and we first went to our church? You went to the little boys' class, and they gave you an hourglass that said, 'Time to pray' on it?"

"Barely," Thomas said, wondering what that had to do with anything.

"Well," his mother continued, "it was found broken behind your bed, and the sand inside of it spread everywhere. It must have been up on your shelf way in the back and then fallen off in whatever commotion was going on in your room."

Again, evidence Thomas could not counter with a story nobody believed.

"The wet mattress then. How did it become soaked night after night?" Thomas asked, thinking he just may have stumped the doubters.

His mother looked at the doctor and then squeezed the police report tighter. Thomas thought his mother always looked sad, but the face she made when Thomas asked about the mattress made Thomas feel like he had severed her heart in two. Thomas instinctively began to feel shame drip from his throat down into his chest, although he did not know why.

"Thomas, the tests show the liquid in your room was urine. It was your urine," said his mother.

"Urine—that can't be," Thomas said softly. "Who did these tests?"

Both his mother and the doctor were silent. Thomas realized that he could not convince anybody to buy his story of the river. Just as science class had taught him, he could not repeat his actions and therefore could not prove them as facts. He made a promise to himself that he would not tell anybody else, ever. Then the door opened.

"The nurse told me he was awake, out of the coma," said a man in a button shirt and dress slacks. When Thomas looked at the man's belt, he saw a shiny police badge and a small black gun. He looked over at Thomas.

"Hey there buddy," he said as if Thomas were a lost dog who finally came home. "I'm Detective Jones."

Thomas looked out into the hallway and saw another full-uniformed policeman standing at his door. "I have it now, Hopkis," Detective Jones said to the officer in the hallway. The officer leaned his head into the room, gave a genuine smile to Thomas, and walked away.

"Mom, I don't understand. The police, these photos and tests—why? It was just a fight. I don't want any trouble for Sketch."

"We aren't here about your fight, Thomas," said the plain-clothes detective as he turned to Thomas's mother to address her. "You said something like this has happened before, right?"

"Yes, well kind of," said Thomas's mother. "They were only allegations. Nothing was ever proven."

"But I understand this time you caught him … well …" Detective Jones spoke softer and began looking back and forth between Thomas and his mother, "… while he was … and that's when you …" He put his arms on Thomas' mother's shoulders. "No, you had to do what you had to do. I have children too and would have done the same thing you did."

Thomas's mother put her hands to her face and began to sob.

"Now, I do understand this wasn't easy to go through," Detective Jones said as he lowered his head to make eye contact with Thomas's mother. "Look at it like this: this is still a situation that can heal with time. I remember one night, when I still did uniform patrol, we received a 911 call, and all the operator could hear on the other line a lady crying hysterically. She never spoke a clear word. Our dispatcher tried to trace the call, but it was a cell phone, so they had to trace it a different way, taking more time.

"Anyway, while the dispatcher was tracing the call, we searched every house in the area where we thought the call was coming from to try to help this poor woman. This went on for an hour; the whole hour she did nothing but cry bitterly. Of course our goal was to solve this lady's problem or at least make whatever was causing the problem to go away. After a little while longer, the dispatcher finally found an exact address and sent us there.

"We came into the house, only to find a mother grieving over her ten-year-old son, who had died from cancer. There was nothing we could have done even if we got to the house the moment we received the call. It's like the lady called for help instinctively, only to realize in mid-dial there was nothing anybody could do. The point I'm trying to make is that when our boys arrived at your apartment, Thomas was still alive, and you took care of the problem for us. Although it's painful, we still have some hope here."

Although Detective Jones intended well, Thomas's mother sobbed as if she didn't hear a word the detective said.

"Why are you crying, Mom?" Thomas asked, feeling more unexplained shame in his chest, as if he caused his mother to cry. "I don't know what's going on, but I didn't mean to do anything bad. Whatever it was, I can fix it. Just don't cry. I'll get out of here, and we'll get Gracie and do something nice and fun. Where is Gracie? Is she with Chuck?"

Thomas's mother looked up at Thomas with glistening, tearful eyes that glimmered from the bright hospital lights. They were the same type of tears that Abraham in the Bible had when he raised the knife to his only son. "Gracie is fine Thomas," she whispered in a raw voice.

"With Chuck, right?" Thomas asked, looking and hoping for some familiar circumstance.

"Honey, Chuck is dead."

CHAPTER 10

AN ANGEL

THOMAS RETURNED TO school two weeks later. Catching up on schoolwork was difficult but not as difficult as diffusing the rumors as to why Thomas had been missing from school. Some said that because of embarrassment Thomas had run away to the big city and his mother had found him selling cigarettes at a circus. Others said Thomas had tried to kill himself, but because he was so stupid, he tried hanging himself by his feet. Even if Thomas took the time to diffuse one person's rumor, ten more would come along with a more twisted version.

Thomas soon learned that the other kids didn't care about the truth, only about the bigger and better rumor. But Thomas cared about the truth; that is, he wanted to know what the truth was. Did he have an adventure on a wild river, both defeating an evil enemy and learning valuable lessons of life and faith, or was it all a wild dream induced by the drugs the doctor had pumped into his body to keep him alive? Of course nobody else could solve this dilemma for Thomas. If he tried to explain it, people would tell him he was crazy, or they would accuse him of lying to get attention. The problem was Thomas's to solve.

Thomas's mother went back to work the day after Thomas came home from the hospital. She had no paid days off, and like she kept saying, "Someone had to pay bills." A girl named Abigail (Abby, everyone called her) came to the house in the morning to watch Gracie now that Chuck was no longer around to contribute. Abby was fifteen years old and had shoulder-length brown hair and brown eyes. She had creamy white skin, which reminded Thomas of a cup of coffee after his mother had poured too much milk into it.

If Thomas were honest with himself, he would admit that she was very pretty, but just like his adventures on the river, Thomas kept his opinion of Abby secret. She came from Thomas's church, just like Frank; only unlike Frank, Abby smiled at Thomas and his mother every time they came to church. Abby's mother educated her at home, making it possible for Abby to come and watch Gracie during the day. This arrangement allowed Abby to earn extra money, which she said she was saving for college, where she wanted to go and study literature.

Anyway, Thomas liked having Abby around because when he came in the door after school, she smiled at him. Thomas didn't know if she smiled knowingly because she understood the whole family situation and had the answers figured out or if she smiled out of cluelessness. Either way, Thomas liked the smile and welcomed it even though he did not show it.

"Hi, Tommy," she said as Thomas walked in the door after school. He hated being called Tommy, but he allowed her to get away with it because of that smile. "How was your school day?"

Thomas did not want to tell her anything other than "fine." But the way she asked him made him feel as if she really wanted to know, as if she really sat there watching Gracie and thinking that her day would not be complete until Thomas came home and shared his day with her. All this plus that smile broke Thomas's will.

"The other kids at school are pretty rough," Thomas began. "They never really liked me anyway."

"I know how that feels," returned Abby, still smiling. "Most other girls my age think I'm strange because I don't go to high school like they do."

Thomas took her words and wrapped them around himself like a cozy blanket. For the first time nearly ever, Thomas felt as if someone else could relate to him. Although against his best judgment, Thomas took a chance with another question.

"Did they ever make up things about you that aren't true?" he asked, rolling his eyes to hide his curiosity.

"Of course they have, Tommy," she responded. "The other girls on my street made up a rumor that all I did was sit in the corner of the house. They thought that because I didn't go to school and speak with other kids, I lost my ability to speak."

"Didn't that bother you," Thomas asked, looking Abby in the eyes.

"Oh no, not really. It got even worse than that," Abby explained. "They also said that not only could I not speak but that I also went blind. Every time I would go outside they would call me Helen Keller and then walk around with their hands out in front of them and make gibberish noises like someone who can't talk."

"Didn't that bother you?" Thomas asked with a small hint of sympathy.

"Not really," Abby said. "I knew it obviously wasn't true. And really the other kids were the ones who looked stupid even though they were trying to make me feel stupid."

Thomas stared at her, in awe of her wisdom.

"Think about it, Tommy," she continued. "If someone believes something about you that you know is not true, who really does that hurt?" She paused few a second to let Thomas have time to think. "It's not you. It's the people who believe the lie because they never get a chance to know the real you, and they miss out on your friendship. Also, if you never let the lies bother you, then how can it do any harm? Think about these things as storms on the river of life; they always come and go, but the river moves on."

Thomas felt punched in the gut, not only by how wise beyond her years Abby sounded but by her last statement.

"What did you just say?" Thomas asked quickly.

"Tommy, didn't you listen?" she said half seriously and half playfully. "I said you can't let the lies people say about you get to you."

"No, no. The river and the storms."

"Oh, yeah ... just think of these things as storms on the river of life," Abby said, partially confused as to why Thomas wanted that part repeated.

Thomas felt a tingling in his body. He felt in his mind what some people call déjà vu (the feeling that you have been somewhere or done something before), except Thomas did not merely feel he had had been somewhere before; he knew he had been. *How could she have known to use those exact words?* Thomas thought to himself.

Thomas felt a force pushing inside of him to tell Abby everything about the Rio Vida, Sal, and everything that had happened to him, but he remembered the promise he made to himself. He knew that Abby would tell her parents and that they would tell people at church. The people at church would then have another reason to talk about Thomas, which would make him to never want to go to church with his mother again, and that would make his mother upset even more. No good. Thomas would have to apply more wit to see if Abby really understood what she had just said.

"Have you ever been to any rivers?" Thomas asked as he raised one eyebrow and tilted his head toward her, feeling rather sleuth-like.

"Well … yeah. My dad takes us camping at least once a year. We usually go somewhere near a river or lake."

"Well, has it ever stormed while you were camping near a river?" Thomas asked anxiously.

"I think one time, why?" she asked.

"Well, what happened when it stormed?" Thomas asked with both eyes wide.

"We got a little wet," Abby said very anticlimactically. "Tommy, I'm not sure what this has to do with our conversation."

"I'm sorry … I just thought maybe you were referring to something else," Thomas said with his shoulders sunk down.

"Like what?" she asked with the same interest in Thomas she expressed before.

"I doubt you would understand," Thomas said. "Not that you're not smart, because I think you are." Thomas wanted to tell her, especially after she had been so comforting to him. Her comfort felt just like hot chocolate on a cold, cloudy day, and Thomas wanted a second helping. But he knew he had to discipline himself and not give in. "It's just a boy thing, I guess."

"That's okay, Tommy. I suppose we all go through different places in our lives. That's what makes each of us unique, right?" she said as she looked at Thomas with her powerful, soothing smile. It was so powerful, in fact, that Thomas felt the whole story rising from his gut through his throat. Just as it was about to exit his mouth like a geyser, the front door opened.

"Mommy," shouted Gracie, who was playing with her dolls during the entire conversation.

Gracie ran into her mother's arms after her mother placed a bag down on the kitchen counter.

"Thomas, grab that bag for me, honey, and put it in my bedroom please," his mother said to him as she hugged Gracie. "Hello, Abby, how did the day go?"

"Very well, Ms. Graves. There were no problems."

Thomas found it strange to hear his mother called by her last name. He never heard his father talk to his mother, and Chuck only called her babe. At church everyone just turned around, said hello, and shook her hand. They never asked her what her name was. Thomas brought the bag into his mother's bedroom just like she asked. He set the bag on the bed and heard a muffled *clink*. This was the same sound the bottles made in the kitchen the night before Thomas fell into his coma. Feeling curious, Thomas looked into the bag.

"These glass bottles are red and are filled with pills," Thomas said under his breath. He pulled one bottle out of the bag and saw his mother's name typed on the label. This was medicine. He tried to pronounce the name bellow his mother's name.

"Tam … tamox … tamoxifen," said Thomas loosely. Thomas put the bottle back in the bag and ran out of the room, hoping to see Abby again just before she left. *Thump* went the door as Thomas came back into the front room.

"Did Abby leave?" he asked his mother, hoping she would say something other than the obvious.

"Yes, honey. Her father just came and picked her up. You know, he is a very polite man." She stopped speaking for a moment and stared up toward the ceiling, as if she spoke to someone else not in the room. "He came to the door and looked at me in the eyes and asked if there was anything that he could do for me. I said no and thanked him, but I really felt that he meant it, like he was sincere about wanting to help." She returned from her trance. "Did you need Abby for something?" asked his mother as her voice cracked with fatigue.

"No, I mean not really," Thomas said, putting his head down. "We were just talking about something."

"She's real nice, isn't she, dear?" his mother said with a weak voice, staring straight ahead as if again she were talking to someone other than Thomas. "Almost like an angel to help in a hard time, right, honey?"

Thomas stared at his mother for a moment, wondering if she was really talking to him. "I don't know about an angel," Thomas said, shrugging his shoulders and faking a laugh, hoping the laugh would mask his true feelings; but it didn't matter. His mother wasn't paying attention. "I know Gracie likes her, and that's good right now."

Thomas started to ask his mother about the pill bottles, but she asked him a question first.

"Can you go and change Gracie's diaper please, Thomas? Phew, she must have been building this stink bomb just for us," she requested.

Thomas took Gracie back to her room. "You know, Mom," he said halfway down the hallway. "I have seen other kids younger than Gracie already potty trained."

"Come on, Thomas," she pleaded. "You know full well why things are different with us. Can you please just help?"

"I know we're different, Mom. I was just saying … I didn't mean to upset you." Thomas knew he said the wrong thing again. He didn't want to say the wrong things. It seemed ever since Thomas woke up in the hospital, his mother had been distant from him. Not that they were close before, but at least earlier Thomas did not feel separated from his mother. Now she treated him as if he were a foster child she did not know but had an obligation to be nice to. Thomas had been saying things to remind her how she used to be before Thomas's coma. He entered Gracie's room.

"Okay, Gracie, lay down," Thomas said as he reached for a new, fresh diaper. "Phew. Why couldn't you have given your stinky to Abby?"

"Abby, Abby," Gracie said with a smile. "I wike Abby."

"So do I," Thomas said in a whisper. "But you can keep my secret, right, Gracie?" Thomas then held his index finger to his lips and made a hush sound.

"Gwace keep Tomish seecwet sssshhhhhhh," she said as she also raised her finger to her lips.

CHAPTER 11

BAD MEDICINE

THOMAS TRUDGED HOME from another day of school filled with other kids and their useless rumors. He tried to apply Abby's advice and not let the lies get to him, but he found out that was like saying don't let the fly on your nose tickle you. Nevertheless, he knew her advice had value because it came from Abby and her smile. Thomas must have misunderstood what it meant to not let the lies get to him. He hurried home to see her.

As he rushed passed all the familiar landmarks, he noticed the empty gas station. He had not thought of it since he got out of the hospital. He remembered how he had always felt a spooky, haunting feeling coming from the station. He recalled how on the river Stainkins had told Thomas that he could see him as he passed the old gas station on his way to school. Thomas pieced a puzzle together, and the picture became clearer. It was Stainkins all those years peering at Thomas through the gas station, creating the haunted feeling.

Thomas understood that adult thinking would conclude that Thomas had got a haunted feeling from the gas station because it was abandoned and that kids fear empty, abandoned structures. Adults would say that because Thomas always had a fear of the gas station, his mind projected those fears into his coma fantasy. The remaining word on the sign was "kins," and Thomas must have created the identity of Jangk Stainkins based on that. Of course, both theories could be correct. Thomas continued home so he could think in the comfort of his apartment.

As he walked home, he thought about telling Abby everything on his mind. He felt so warm with her yesterday, but did that mean he could trust her? His mother, the doctor, and every other adult said that Thomas had a wild dream. Abby was older than Thomas, but she was not yet an adult. Maybe she could and would understand Thomas's dilemma. Thomas arrived at the front door, bursting through.

"Oh Tommy, good thing you're here," said Abby, who sat in the front room, only without her smile. In fact, her eyes seemed sad, and her lips were flat and tight, with a slight curve downward at each end, making a small frown. Gracie was playing with her toys next to Abby, seemingly unaffected by whatever made Abby sad. "Your mom was taken home by some people from her work. They said she should go to the hospital, but she refuses to go."

Thomas looked down the hall and noticed his mother's purse on the floor, and he saw her closed bedroom door.

"What happened to her?" Thomas asked with a blank face.

"Her coworkers said she could not stop throwing up. Of course they were concerned, but at the same time they can't have someone puking inside a restaurant. I offered to stay here and help out until Gracie goes to bed. I already called my dad."

Thomas remembered what his mom said about needing to pay the bills, and suddenly his own problems felt small. He knew that his visit to the hospital had produced a tidal wave of bills that flooded his mother. No wonder she did not want to go to the hospital for herself. Thomas began to feel more shame pouring down his throat and into his chest; his eyes welled up with tears. He could not let Abby see tears in his eyes, so he went into his room and shut the door without saying another word to her.

Thomas dried his eyes in his room and then checked on his mother. She slept strangely in her bed, provoking Thomas's curiosity. Her shallow breaths alerted him. He had heard her sleeping deeply before, but this was different. When she inhaled, it sounded like a swimmer taking a quick breath before submerging, and when she exhaled, it sounded like the rush of air someone lets out when she has been punched in the stomach. Even worse, she would sometimes go almost twenty seconds before taking another breath. He tried waking her by poking her with his finger, but she did not respond. He then jostled her with one hand but still nothing. He then used both hands shaking her vigorously—nothing. Thomas felt stiff with fear because of his lack of knowledge to do anything helpful. Desperate for knowledge, Thomas ran to the front room to ask Abby for help.

"I can't get her to wake up," Thomas said, rounding the corner to the front room.

"Why are you trying to wake her?" Abby questioned Thomas with concern. "She needs her sleep if she felt that badly."

"But she's not sleeping normal. She sounds like one of those semi trucks when they downshift gears on the highway."

"Well, we should probably call paramedics if you think she is that bad."

Abby called 911.

"What are you waiting for?" Thomas pleaded. "Tell them they need to hurry and check on my mom."

"I'm on hold, Tommy," Abby said, raising her shoulders, indicating that there was nothing that she could do.

"911 put you on hold?" asked Thomas, baffled. "That doesn't make any sense."

Feeling anxious, Thomas could not wait by the phone. He went down the hallway and waited outside his mother's door. He felt too scared to go inside the room. He feared not knowing what to do if his mother's condition worsened. *What if she vomited and started choking?* he thought. Even worse, what would Thomas do if his mother stopped breathing altogether?

He remembered the CPR lessons from health class, or at least he remembered going to the class. All he recalled was that you were supposed to push on someone's chest if they didn't have a heartbeat. In the middle of the lesson, Thomas wondered what one was supposed to do if a woman did not have a heartbeat. Of course he knew it was wrong to touch a woman on the chest, and therefore, it became a moral math problem in his twelve-year-old mind. His mind stopped listening to the lesson to try to solve the moral problem, and he never learned the practical applications of CPR. Thomas leaned against the wall, sliding his back down it until his backside hit the floor. He wrapped his arms around his legs burying his head into his knees, and sobbed lightly.

Minutes later, Thomas heard the echo of sirens in the distance getting louder. Finally the siren became so loud Thomas thought the ambulance had driven through the apartment building. The siren suddenly shut off, but the lights still rotated, causing Thomas's apartment to look like a carnival at night.

"A firetwuck," Gracie said from the front room.

"Yes, honey," Abby said to her in return. At first Thomas felt angry that Gracie didn't understand what was happening; he felt that Abby seemed to conceal that her mother was ill. Then it occurred to him that Gracie's blissful ignorance would be easier to manage.

Next Thomas heard Abby opening the front door. "Over there in the back," he heard her say to the paramedics.

"Excuse us, bud," said a large man dressed in blue-and-yellow puffy pants with a tight blue t-shirt with the words "Fire Department" on it. He was carrying a plastic box that was about three feet long and a foot tall. Thomas saw that it had monitors and dials and buttons just like the machines he remembered from the hospital. Thomas felt that the paramedic spoke to him like he didn't grasp the seriousness of the situation. Thomas preached of the seriousness.

"I tried to wake her up, but she wouldn't," Thomas said with emphasis, but he felt his words fall off his mouth and onto the floor. The paramedics did not acknowledge him.

"Hey buddy," said one of the paramedics, not looking at Thomas. "Do me a favor and wait out in the front room with your sisters. Can ya?" He then knelt down by Thomas's mother and began fastening a strap around her arm.

Thomas felt violated. *This is my mother,* he thought, *and they have no right to put their hands on her without me being here.* Of course Thomas didn't say this to the paramedics. He walked to the front room as he had been asked. Abby and Gracie sat on the couch saying nothing. He heard the paramedics still working.

"Get the Narcan," one said.

"Is this an overdose?" asked the other.

"I don't know," said the first paramedic. "It looks like she's taking these for the pain of her condition. They are prescription; she just may have taken too much."

"Hey, I remember this lady … that's right in this very apartment. She's the one that off'ed that guy who was in that kid's room …"

"Shut your mouth, genius. That's the same kid out there."

Two more paramedics came in, wheeling a gurney into his

mother's room, and then they wheeled his mother out and into an ambulance downstairs. Thomas could hear his mother groaning as they took her out, indicating she was still alive. Abby called her father, and he came to pick up the children. He drove Abby and Gracie back to his home and then drove Thomas to the hospital to find out about his mother. Abby's father's name was Ken, and he stood about six foot even and had dark hair. He did not have a big, muscular build, but his sharply defined face made him look masculine and strong—yet his smooth brown eyes and consistent smile made him approachable.

"Stay here," he said to Thomas as they entered the hospital. "I'm going to try to get some information." Thomas took a seat just outside of the gift shop. He looked over at the glass window and saw the large flower displays with bright, beautiful colors and felt comforted by them. He then looked and saw the cards that went with the flowers and saw phases like, "*Sorry for your loss*" written on the cards. A sharp feeling struck Thomas in the stomach like a punch. Of course Thomas had feared for his mother's well-being before, but Thomas realized he sat in the building where he might lose his mother forever. This thought numbed his whole body and brought tears to his eyes.

"Thomas," said Abby's father, "they said that they stabilized her and that we can see her in a few minutes." He stopped and noticed Thomas's tears. "Oh Thomas, I'm not going to tell you to relax, and I'm not going to tell you that everything will be okay. But we will figure this out together." He said this with a flat smile, the kind that shows sensitivity in tough times, not with a wide, clown smile that shows a lack of understanding.

Thomas looked up at him. Ken was sincere, and it sounded strange. Thomas thought it sounded strange. Most people from the church would say something like, "It will be all right" as they patted you on the shoulder, and then they would turn and talk to someone else.

"What do you mean by all that?" Thomas asked, wiping the tears out of his eyes.

"What I mean is that I don't know what will be the outcome of your mother's condition. It would be foolish of me to tell you that everything will be all right when I don't know that." Ken's eyes seemed to travel directly into Thomas's soul. Thomas did not know Abby's father much at all, but his manner toward Thomas produced an instant trust. "Right now," he continued, "you may feel a bunch of different emotions. I couldn't tell you which one is the right one to feel. They're your feelings."

"I feel scared right now," Thomas said, looking up at Ken.

"I would too."

"I … I don't want her to die," Thomas said while trying to swallow the baseball-sized lump of fear and sadness lodged in his throat.

"Well," said Ken, pausing for a moment and trying to find the words to explain life to someone else's kid, "someday she will."

Thomas looked up at him, knowing Ken's sincerity, but giving him a look that indicated that his words weren't very comforting.

"Thomas, I know you're young, but you're not a little child anymore. To say that everyone dies is like saying everyone breathes." Ken lifted his shoulders and hands as if to apologize for explaining the obvious. "But for some reason, even though everyone knows death is part of life, people get personally offended when death happens close to them."

Thomas stared at Ken, letting him know he had not yet comforted Thomas.

"I guess what I'm trying to say, Thomas, is that nothing in your life happens to you for the specific purpose of causing you personal harm. Everything that happens happens because you're alive in this world, and everyone living here will experience more or less the same things in some form or another. What makes a difference in people is how they handle the same storms we all go through on the river of life."

Thomas saw the hospital hallway collapse, allowing him to see only Ken's head. He had heard Abby talk about storms and the river of life. That one time could have been a coincidence, but to hear these exact words twice made Thomas believe it was no coincidence. "What did you just say?" Thomas asked Abby's father in a cautious whisper.

"What part Thomas? We have been talking about many things," Ken asked.

"The river," Thomas said impatiently, as if Ken had dangled a juicy cheeseburger in front of a starving Thomas. "The part about the river and the storms. Abby said those very words the other day, and now you just said them."

"Oh," Ken said with a small chuckle. "I use that phrase to explain things to her all the time. She must have just been repeating me."

Perhaps thinking about his mother's sickness caused Thomas to drop his guard, but he felt maybe Abby's father knew more about Thomas's journeys than he let on. Thomas remembered Sal and how he felt when Sal seemed to be someone more than he presented himself to be. He began to think the same thoughts about Ken. He felt as if pretending he never went to the river was like pretending he did not need to eat. He could ignore the hunger for a while, but eventually, the pangs and the weakness would nag him, reminding him of the truth that he needed food. He felt that denying that he ever went to the river caused him the same pangs and weakness, but of his spirit. Believing Ken must have known something special, Thomas decided to break his promise and tell Ken about the river.

"Ken, can I call you Ken … sir?" Thomas asked, using Ken's name, believing it produced confidence. "Have you ever been to the Rio V—"

"Thomas, I can take you and your guest back to see your mother now," interrupted a nurse who had just walked up to Thomas and Ken, cutting off Thomas's chances.

Thomas hesitated. He saw Ken staring at Thomas intently, as if he were a catcher in a baseball game waiting for Thomas's pitch. But the nurse hovered over both of them, intimidating Thomas from saying anything about the river out loud.

"Okay," said Thomas. "Let's go see her." He walked away, looking forward and then staring up at Ken as if Ken were on a train Thomas missed, and Thomas watched as Ken's train left the station. The nurse led them around the emergency room, eventually coming to the bed that cradled Thomas's mother. Arriving at the bed, Ken stopped at the edge of the curtain, and then he nodded at Thomas to let him know that this visit was for Thomas alone.

"Honey," his mother said in a raspy voice. "Are you okay? Where is Gracie?" She held out her hand to touch Thomas.

"She's fine, Mom," Thomas explained as he grabbed her hand. "She's with Abby at her house. What's the matter with you?"

"I'll explain that later, at home hopefully," she said as she looked up toward the nurse who was tending the IV line. The nurse said nothing but returned a smile and tilted her head toward Thomas's mother. "I do have to stay the night here, they say for observation." His mother then looked up over toward Abby's father, and she opened her mouth to speak.

"I'll take Thomas home with me tonight," Ken said before Thomas's mother had a chance to ask. "Little Gracie can sleep in

Abby's room since she's comfortable with her, and Thomas can use the one of the spare bedrooms." Thomas's mother put her head back into the pillow and relaxed her shoulders. She mouthed the words *thank you* to Ken without speaking out loud.

Thomas went home in the car with Ken. He felt too intimidated to bring up the conversation they were having before seeing Thomas's mother. Thomas began to attribute the same mystery to Abby's father as he did to Sal—that Ken too represented something greater. Although intimidated, Thomas thirsted for conversation with Ken about the river. He made several week attempts to start the conversation, almost like someone trying to start an avalanche with a whisper on a snowy mountain.

"Thanks for helping me tonight," Thomas said. "I enjoyed talking with you, especially in the hospital hallway." Thomas felt that if Ken truly understood the significance of storms on the river then he would know exactly what Thomas was referring to when he said "the conversation in the hallway."

"Do you like the smell of commercial-grade cleaner?" Ken asked, looking oddly at Thomas, indicating that he did not quite understand the reference.

"No I mean …" Thomas began to say that he referred to the river, but he stopped himself, perceiving that Ken did not understand. Thomas realized he would be in a dangerous place if he spoke any more about the river without Ken understanding. "I mean it was just nice to have you there with me, that's all," Thomas said, frustrated.

Later at Abby's house, Thomas lay down in the spare room. The bed had crisp new sheets that smelled flowery, the bed felt soft, and the room was perfectly air conditioned. Thomas's body felt comfortable, but his soul felt displaced. The comfort gave Thomas more time to think about how strange his life had become. His mother's mystery illness, Chuck's death, and the dream about the river all clouded Thomas's mind like a thick fog, leaving no room for other thoughts. He fell asleep mumbling.

"God, I don't understand … I don't … I don't … I doubt …"

CHAPTER 12

SPANISH LESSON

"WAKE UP, WAKE up, wake up."

Thomas woke suddenly to Gracie pounding on his chest. He picked her up and walked out into the breakfast nook at Abby's house.

"Sorry, Tommy," Abby said. She flashed her smile like a badge that stated she had the authority to comfort, diffusing any grumpiness Thomas had. "We sent her in because we figured you would be used to her rather than any of us." Thomas could not disagree with Abby and her smile.

"We're not sure how long you're mother will be in the hospital," said Abby's mother, who looked just like Abby, only older and taller. "So we thought you should probably get up and go to school, and we will come get you if anything changes."

"My mom said she would be out of the hospital by today," Thomas reassured her with confidence. Abby's mother looked at Thomas, tilted her head, and smiled at Thomas in the same way the nurse looked at Thomas's mother when his mother said the same thing in the hospital.

"We'll see what happens, dear," she said, looking at the floor while making a flat smile with her lips.

Thomas got dressed with some clothes Abby's family kept around for the times her male cousins would come over. Thomas pulled the crisp shirt over his body; it smelled fresh, like it just came from the store. Thomas looked at himself in the mirror after he was completely dressed in the new clothes and thought that he had never looked nicer. He went back out into the main room, where Abby and her mother were and prepared to go to school.

"Thomas, I can drive you to school," said Abby's mother with a tone of charity in her voice.

"No thanks, I know where I am, and I can walk. It helps me to walk," he said as he looked at her and then looked at the floor, feeling he had looked at her long enough. "But when my mom gets released, you can pick me up … if you could."

Abby's mother nodded at Thomas in agreement.

"Abby," Thomas said as he lowered his voice and turned his face toward her, "when your dad would talk to you about your problems being like storms on the river, what did he say to do during the storms?"

"Well," Abby began as she tilted her head upward, looking for the precise answer, "he usually says something about the storm testing your work and your faith."

"What does that mean?" Thomas asked, puzzled.

"I know, Tommy," she said reassuringly, "he always talks with these comparisons to some place with this river as if he had been there, and I have a hard time understanding too."

With a spiked interest, he looked at Abby more intensely. *Could this possibly be?* he thought to himself. Thomas thought Ken knew more than he was telling.

"He says," she continued, "that the storms will test the structure of your life and how well you have built it."

"Did he say what kind of structures?" he asked even though his lips were numb from anxiety.

"I'm not sure," she said, tilting her head because she was puzzled by Thomas's question. "Why does the type of structure matter?"

"It just does," Thomas said impatiently. "What about the faith? What does he mean by testing your faith?"

"Well, he said as long as your faith is tied down to the right source, then no storm can do you much harm." As she said these things, she watched Thomas's jaw drop and his face turn bright, as if she were chanting a magic spell she did not herself understand.

"Did he say 'tie down'? Did he use those words, and did he say you tie it with a rope? What does the right source mean … God … Jesus … what?" Thomas pelted Abby with questions.

"I mean," she said, feeling slightly uncomfortable, not understanding Thomas's excitement, "he never said rope, but I assumed that's what you tie something with." She paused to take a breath. "And God and Jesus, well yeah. I mean, what else are we supposed to have faith in?" She looked up at the clock. "Oh Tommy, look at the time! You need to get to school."

Thomas got up from the chair feeling drenched with numbness— the kind one feels upon hearing good or bad news. He walked to the door and then turned around before he went out. "What do you know about the old gas station that's on the way to school, the one with the sign that says 'kins' on it?"

Abby stared at him for a second as she collected her thoughts, wondering why Thomas had become so excited and wondering what relevance the old gas station had. "I don't know anything about it, Tommy, but the library keeps all the property records for all the buildings in town."

"Excellent. Thanks, Abby," he said with a well-intentioned, mischievous smile and then went out the door. Thomas went to school feeling like a brand new boy. He had confidence in himself, as if his nagging feelings about the river were correct even though no one else believed him. Thomas had the edge for once. But if Ken did know about the Rio Vida and the Santa Fe and the whole river experience, then why did he act like he did not? Thomas had no answer for that question, but that did not deter his confidence.

He passed the old gas station, looking into it as he passed by with a confident curiosity rather than fear. "I'll figure you out after school," he said under his breath.

Thomas beckoned the end of the school day as a child would an ice cream truck coming down the street. He looked at the clock every thirty seconds, making the school day longer. Thomas made it all the way to the last class, Spanish. The room was painted blood red and had strange statues and face masks of skeletons. This led Thomas to believe that Spanish was a violent, scary language, and he wanted no part of it, especially now that the skeletons reminded him of Jangk Stainkins. He usually paid no attention to the class, but on this day, something about the lesson caught Thomas's ear. Mrs. Contrero taught the class. She was a short, round woman who wore bright, skin-tight pants, which Thomas found unpleasant. When she didn't feel like teaching, she played classic Spanish romantic records or showed Spanish soap operas. Thomas preferred the records. Anyway, today's lesson was vocabulary.

"*Levantan se,*" she said, causing most of the class to stand up out of their chairs. Thomas guessed that the word must mean stand and stood. Mrs. Contrero then waddled her feet in a circle to turn her short, chubby body around to face the chalkboard and began to write words in two columns, one in Spanish and the other in

English. She also explained that Spanish had come from Latin, which is an ancient language spoken in Roman times.

"*Dia,*" said the class in unison as Mrs. Contrero pointed to the word in the column. "Day," they said as she then pointed to the English column. Thomas figured out that the English word was the equivalent of the Spanish word and that dia in Spanish meant day in English. *That was pretty simple,* Thomas thought.

"*Hora,*" said the class again all together as Mrs. Contrero pointed to the Spanish column, and "hour," they said in English.

"Not so hard," Thomas mumbled to himself, feeling an unfamiliar confidence in his ability to comprehend concepts.

"*Rio,*" said the class in chorus. Thomas's ears stuck up like a dog who had just heard a familiar call. This was part the river's name: the Rio Vida. Mrs. Contrero then pointed to the English column. "River," everyone spoke together. *Of course,* Thomas thought to himself, *that makes sense.* The Rio Vida was a river; why shouldn't that be part of its name?

The rotund teacher pointed to the next Spanish word. "*Muerte,*" everyone said aloud, and then the teacher pointed to the English word, "Death." *Just like this room,* Thomas thought to himself, still staring at the skeletons. Then the next word came.

"*Vida,*" shouted the class. Thomas felt the room close in around him so that all he could see in his line of vision was the word "vida" written on the chalkboard. Thomas knew that the English meaning came next. What had been taking only a few seconds had turned into eternity. He saw Mrs. Contrero's hand motion toward the English column. He looked around him and compared the rest of the class to jurors in a trial who were about to announce Thomas's sentence. "Life," they all spoke clearly and crisply. *That's what it means?* Thomas asked himself in his thoughts. *Vida means life. The Rio Vida, the River of Life.* Thomas found these events to be far more than a coincidence. Now what about Santa Fe, what did that mean? The rest of the class faded into a blur. After class, Thomas approached Mrs. Contrero's desk.

"Mrs. Contrero," Thomas said humbly, still numb from his revelation of the meaning of Rio Vida.

"Senora Contrero," she snapped at Thomas, reminding him of her preference to addressed by her Spanish title.

"Sorry, Senora," Thomas said after he had taken a step backward.

"*Esta bien,* Thomas," she said with a smile that contradicted her earlier irritation. "*Que quieres,* what do you want, Thomas?" she asked.

"Well, Senora, I was wondering if you could help me understand some words," he said hesitantly, not wanting to offend her again. "Do you know what Santa Fe means?" he asked, hesitantly not sure if it was a Spanish phase. He figured that if Rio Vida was Spanish then Santa Fe must be also—at least it sounded Spanish to Thomas.

"Oh, Thomas, *que bueno,*" she screeched with a happy, high-pitched screech. Not knowing exactly what was going on, Thomas smiled to put himself in accord with Mrs. Contrero. "Are you Catholic?" she asked.

"No," said Thomas, flattening out his smile because the question confused him.

"Oh," she said, lowering her enthusiasm. "Have you ever lived in New Mexico?" she asked.

"No, Ma'am, I mean Senora," Thomas said in return.

"Oh, well. Santa Fe means holy faith in English. Does that help you?" she asked, returning to an unenthusiastic state.

"Yes Ma'am, I mean Senora. It does help. Thank you so much." Thomas walked out of the classroom with more information than he knew what to do with.

"So I was on the river of life and I had to go underneath it to find holy faith." Thomas spoke out loud as he walked away from the school and toward the town library. Even if the river trip actually took place, what did it mean in light of all this new information? Thomas did not see Abby's mother waiting for him outside the school. This meant that his mom had not yet been released from the hospital. "Oh well," Thomas thought out loud. He felt it meant that the doctors were taking extra precautions with her. *Not a problem,* he thought. *They will release her.* Now he had proof that his dream was more than imagined.

Thomas arrived at the library and asked the librarian where the property records were kept. She pointed out the place and left Thomas by himself to find exactly what he was looking for. He searched through the section that stated, "Main Street." Rifling through the files, he found nothing under K for Kins, the name written on the sign above the service station. He then remembered what Stainkins told Thomas on the river, and with a creepy hunch, Thomas looked under the letter S.

A cold, spider-like shiver crawled up his spine when the first file he saw was labeled "Stainkins Service Station." Thomas slowly pulled out the file from the drawer and carried it over to the table. *The smoking gun,* thought Thomas to himself. *Now I know I have been to the river, and this Stainkins file will prove it. How else would I have known about Stainkins's name?* It was too strange of a name to be a coincidence. Thomas realized he had sabotaged himself. He never told anyone about Stainkins. They would think that he merely read the name on the file and added it to his wild river story. Nevertheless, Thomas had proved to himself that his dream had merit.

Thomas dug into the file and pulled out documents the local bank dated January 6, 1945. It stated Jangk Johann Stainkins received a loan for his service station. Stainkins had served in the army and fought in the Normandy D-day invasion. He was wounded and discharged, and then he took out a veteran's loan to start his business.

"Stainkins was a war hero?" Thomas muttered in unbelief. He dug deeper into the file, finding another official-looking document. "Divorce Decree" the paper stated. It said that Jangk Johann Stainkins officially divorced Mini Petunia Stainkins; reason, infidelity of wife. Thomas had to use the dictionary to look up the word infidelity. He learned it meant one partner in marriage did not honor the commitment to the other partner. Another bank document stated that the business had been awarded to Stainkins's wife in the divorce.

"How could his wife get his business if she caused the divorce?" Thomas said softly, realizing he sat in a library. He dug deeper into the file and found a newspaper clipping dated July 28, 1948. It stated the following:

> A terrible fire broke out at the Stainkins Service Station on Main Street early this morning, claiming one life, which investigators believe to be the owner, Mr. Jangk Stainkins. It is unknown why Mr. Stainkins was inside the business in the early morning. Police are unsure if foul play is involved. A statement from his estranged wife, Mrs. Petunia Stainkins, was read by her attorney, Mr. Kirk Stainkins, who ironically is the owner's brother.

"That just doesn't seem right," Thomas said out loud. He dug deeper and found a police report of the incident authored by an Officer Flannigan. It stated:

On July 28, 1948, I was dispatched by the desk sergeant to a fire at the Stainkins Service Station at 1524 Main Street to assist the fire department with traffic control. After performing my traffic control duties, I was summoned by the fire chief to observe the charred remains of a body that was on the floor in the middle of the station. I observed that the body had been burned beyond immediate identification. I noticed that the arms of the body were up against the neck and that the hands were clinched in a grasping manner. I looked around the area and immediately, above the body, I observed a rope tied to the main beam of the building. The rope had been scorched. It was unclear if the rope had been tied around the body on the ground. I then notified the desk sergeant of the body, and the county detective unit came out to take disposition of the scene.

"No wonder he was so angry," Thomas said out loud. "He seemed to have been fighting his whole life and just couldn't stop." Thomas put the documents back in the folder and walked back to the file cabinet.

"Thomas," said a muffled female's voice. Thomas saw nobody at first but then saw Abby walking toward him. He did not expect to see Abby; she had always called him Tommy. As she got closer, Thomas saw that Abby did not smile.

"What is it, Abby?" Thomas asked in a hushed tone.

"I thought you might be here," she said nervously as she rubbed her hands together. "My mom and I drove the route to your school, and then we went to your apartment. I remembered that you had asked about the library earlier, so we came here."

Thomas perceived Abby's nervousness. "What's wrong? Why would you come looking for me?" Thomas remembered his mother in the hospital. He had been so excited about his discoveries that he had forgot about her. "Oh, my mom," he said with relief, believing she was ready to be released. "Are we going to go get her now from the hospital?"

At first Abby didn't say anything. "Yes, we do need to go to the hospital," she said as she grabbed Thomas's hand, turned around, and walked toward the exit.

This was the first time he held a girl's hand other than his mother's. Thomas felt as if his whole body were dipped in a warm, comforting bath. Her soft, smooth, warm hands were the opposite of his mother's, which felt rough, cold, and clammy. Thomas spied the middle of Abby's back and saw how slender and petite she looked, and yet, he felt the strength in her grip. She reminded him of a deer—so small and frail looking but very powerful and swift. Her smooth brown hair swayed from left to right as she walked, mesmerizing Thomas lulling him into a trance. This trance prevented Thomas from noticing that Abby's mother was crying as he got in the car.

"Thomish," said Gracie, who was in her car seat reaching out toward Thomas.

"Gracie!" Thomas said in return as he grabbed her arm and hugged her head in big brother fashion. "Stop eating your boogers," Thomas said slightly louder than normal, looking to get a small chuckle out of both Abby and her mother.

But they did not chuckle; they seemed to not hear what Thomas said. Thomas then came out of his Abby-induced high and saw the long faces of both women. He noticed that Abby's mother was biting her lip and that her shoulders would flinch back every few seconds as she breathed rapidly through her nose.

Thomas reached toward Abby's knee to get her attention, but he decided he should shake her shoulder instead. She looked at him, and Thomas saw the tear-pregnant brown eyes hovering above the strong frown. At first Thomas felt he had done something wrong and began to feel guilty without knowing what he did.

"What's the matter?" Thomas mouthed with a tiny whisper, attempting to keep his investigation low key.

But Abby did not say anything; she put her head in her hands and sobbed. Reviewing the last twenty four hours, Thomas could not recall one incident for which he should be in trouble. He slowly realized that his mother must be worse then he thought. The sad fog from the girls crept onto Thomas; it traveled first from his legs to his chest and finally to his eyes. The tears welled up, and he made every effort not to release them in front of Abby. But one tear escaped and slowly trickled down his cheek. It was the left cheek, the same side Abby sat on. Thomas thought he should quickly brush the tear back, as if he were scratching an itch, but he felt it wise to bring no attention to the tear as everyone was occupied by their own sadness. Thomas's efforts to camouflage his tear were in vain. Abby's hand gently removed the tear from his check; then she dropped her hand into Thomas's and caressed it with the same gentle firmness she had done before.

"Thank you," Thomas whispered through a grief-clogged throat.

CHAPTER 13

BLACK CLOUD DAY

ABBY'S MOTHER DROVE into the hospital parking lot. Thomas unbuckled Gracie, the only person in the vehicle with dry eyes.

"See Mommy," she said as she leaped out of the car seat holding Thomas's hand.

"Yeah, see Mommy," Thomas repeated to her as he wiped his eye and sniffled.

They entered the hospital, and Abby's mother went to the information window. After Abby's mother whispered something to the nurse, she sat up immediately and Abby's mother returned to the group.

"They have a separate room for us," Abby's mom said to Thomas. He wondered why they could not go and see his mother like they had the night before. *She must be much worse and needs her rest,* he thought to himself.

The nurse reemerged and ushered them to a private room to the side of the main waiting room. As Thomas passed through the door, he saw two male figures; the first was a man in a long white coat, whom Thomas assumed was a doctor. The second man was Pastor Phil from Thomas's church. Thomas found the doctor's presence natural, but he did not understand why Pastor Phil was in the room.

Thomas knew Pastor Phil and liked him. Pastor Phil was about sixty-five years old with grey, balding hair. He walked with a limp, which he had acquired as an army chaplain during the Vietnam War. He prayed with Thomas's mother every week when she went up the aisle. As far as Thomas knew, Pastor Phil was the only man who did not treat his mother badly or make her cry. Thomas liked him, but he still did not understand the need for his presence at the hospital.

"Thomas … son," said Pastor Phil as he reached out and touched Thomas on the shoulder, speaking in a low, gruff voice, as if John Wayne played the part of Pastor Phil, "I need to talk to you about your mother."

"Why can't I just see her?" Thomas asked, comforted yet intimidated.

"Well," the pastor paused for a moment, "you'll see her in just a bit, and you can see her later too. Much later, and with so much more joy." Thomas stared at him blankly. The battle-hardened pastor who had comforted dying solders found speaking to a twelve-year-old boy about his mother far more difficult. "Thomas, you mother passed away this morning at ten thirty."

Thomas's body went numb—not the comfortable numb but the numb one's arm or leg feels when one has been sleeping on it and it feels like a million needles inside. "Passed away" struck a blow to Thomas, yet it still wasn't clear. Passed away sounds too soft of a term, almost like deep sleep or coma, a term that still contains a small amount of hope. Thomas thought maybe passed away meant very sick.

"When will she recover?" Thomas asked with a dim hope.

Pastor Phil reconsidered his words, deciding Thomas needed to hear some absolutes. "Son, she died today, and she can't come back." He paused again to let the word died sink in. "But you will be able to go and see her someday," the pastor added, attempting to add a positive edge to death.

The death bomb thrown by the pastor covered Thomas with a deeper numbness. He waited a moment to let the numbness clear and then spoke. "I don't understand," Thomas said as he shook his head in denial. "She only had a stomachache. How could that kill her?"

The doctor in the white coat spoke. "Thomas, your mother had been sick for a long time. She had cancer in her breast."

"Cancer," Thomas repeated in unbelief.

"Yes," continued the doctor, "we had been trying to shrink it with various methods, but it was very aggressive and spread fast, weakening her body."

"But she always said we had no money. How could she have been doing that?" Thomas asked, hearing himself talk as if it were someone else's voice.

"Your church has been paying for the bills, but sometimes the best care in the world cannot stop a deadly disease." The doctor kneeled down to the same level as the pastor. "We gave her the best we had, son. It was just her time."

Gracie had hopped out of Abby's mother's lap and waddled over to Thomas. She put her arms around his back. "Thomish sad?" she asked.

Thomas looked down on her, and he understood how Gracie had lived up to her name. She truly was the graceful one. Of course she did not understand the significance of the events, but she probably never would. She had been spared from much of the pain from her mother's death, and in time she might not remember it at all. She had been watched by so many other people her whole young life that she did not find it strange her mother had been gone and had not yet come back.

Thomas was different. He had been around his mother all twelve years of his life except when she was working, and for him the change would be great. He thought of their apartment and how they would never be there together again. He thought of how distant his mother had become to him in the last few weeks and how he would never have a chance to regain that closeness. He wanted so badly to convince her of his experience on the Rio Vida, and now his chance was gone. Thomas felt these thoughts becoming tears. He felt the pastor tighten his grip on Thomas's shoulder as a sign of comfort; he also felt the soft, firm hand of Abby on his back.

"Thomas," said the doctor in a soft voice, "your sister is too young, but you're old enough to come back and see your mother's body if you feel you up to it. Your pastor and friends here can come with you."

"I don't know," said Thomas between sobs. He found it strange that the doctor referred to Thomas's mother as a body, as if it were only a possession of hers and not really her. He had never seen a dead body before, and he was not sure that he wanted his mother to be the first dead person he saw.

"It's your choice, Thomas," said Pastor Phil. "If you don't want to, everybody understands."

"No," Thomas said and then paused for a bit. "I need to. Everyone else will see her later, and I don't want to be part of a crowd. I want to show her I find her more special then that." He turned to Abby. "Will you come with me?" he asked with tear-filled eyes.

"I ... I ... can't. It just would be too strange—"

"I'll go in with you, honey," said Abby's mother to Thomas. "Abby will stay here with Gracie." Thomas knew Abby didn't say no to hurt him. He understood the strangeness of the situation.

"Okay, I'm ready," he stated after a few moments of regaining a loose control over his emotions. Abby's mother took Thomas by the shoulder, rubbing it up and down as they followed the doctor back through the ER and into a room marked "viewing." Thomas watched as the doctor opened the door and held it open just enough so they could all enter without a crowd seeing inside.

Thomas felt fear come over his body. He knew his mother would not rise up and grab at him; he wished she would. That would be far less scary than seeing her lifeless. He closed his eyes as Abby's mother guided him inside. Thomas once rode a roller coaster with his eyes closed to lessen the fear of the coming loop on the track. By the time the coaster hit the loop, Thomas had to ride it out; seeing the obstacle approaching brought on the majority of the fear. Thomas used this strategy to view his mother's body.

He heard the door close and knew the time had come to open his eyes. He started slowly, knowing a full-blown image might be too much to handle at first. Through the small slats in his eyes, he saw a pair of motionless feet. Then he opened his eyes a little wider and saw the motionless legs and torso covered in a hospital gown. Thomas had feared of seeing his mother's lifeless face, but he had gone too far and could not stop now. Abby's mother continued to stroke his back up and down, giving him a small amount of strength; that's all he needed. He moved his eyes across the torso and then to the chest. Out of the corner of his eye, he could see his mother's blurry face, but at this point, it could still be anybody's. He took a deep breath, swallowed the lump of fear lodged in his throat, and focused his eyes on his mother's lifeless face.

"She looks so beautiful," Thomas said in a whisper. He thought his mother looked like she did in old photographs before Thomas was born. With her eyes shut and her mouth closed in neither a smile nor a frown, she appeared to be only sleeping peacefully. Instead of a stressed-out, overworked mother, he saw a fair young woman whose wrinkles had smoothed out and whose ragged hair had softened. He saw that she did not have the stress of going to work and paying the bills. Thomas knew he could not disturb her any more with his problems. He reached out to touch her cheek and felt the cold lifelessness of her body, confirming that she was gone.

"I love her so much still," he said as he burst into heavy tears, still touching his mother's cheek. Abby's mother came from behind and put her right arm around Thomas's body and her left around his forehead, pulling him into her chest. Thomas did not know, but she also had burst into tears. Pastor Phil knelt down next to Thomas and grabbed hold of his free hand; his eyes were closed. After an unknown amount of time, they left the room together, Abby's mother still embracing Thomas's shoulder and Pastor Phil still holding his hand. As they went through the door, Thomas saw the doctor cover his mother's head with a sheet. And then the door closed.

When they returned to the private waiting room Thomas saw that Ken had joined Abby and Gracie. He held Abby's head to his shoulder because she was crying as Gracie played on the floor. When Ken saw Thomas walk in, he held out his hand to him, indicating he desired Thomas to come near. He looked at Thomas with a flat, sympathetic smile but said nothing. Thomas walked over to him and sat down.

"She's gone over the waterfall, Ken," he said, looking straight ahead, not looking for a response. Ken just put his arm around Thomas's shoulder and squeezed. Thomas didn't see Ken's face.

"I need to leave now," said the doctor. "But if you have any questions, Thomas, please send for me. I'll do what I can to make time for you." Thomas looked up at him and nodded his head in thanks with tear-thick eyes.

"Do you have the legal issues handled?" the doctor asked Abby's parents. They both nodded their heads. Thomas assumed the doctor spoke of Thomas' living arrangements and believed he would be staying at Abby's house for a while. After regaining their composure, they left the waiting room.

The drive home seemed take place in another world. They drove out of the same hospital parking lot and passed the same trees and buildings, but it was all different now. There was no hope in any of these landmarks. Thomas saw them on the way to the hospital, but he saw them in a realm of hope, with a hint of possibility that he might pass them on the way home with his mother next to him. But now that was no longer possible. *I suppose this is quite a storm on my river,* Thomas thought to himself. The storm clouds rolled in, removing the color and making everything black and white—mostly black.

CHAPTER 14

NO REASON NOT TO

NOT THAT THOMAS needed more storms, but he and Gracie did not live with Abby's family as he had expected. Abby's grandmother became very ill and needed to live at Abby's house; they had no room for both a three-year-old and twelve-year-old orphan. Of course the government stepped in and placed the children in an approved foster home. The foster parents were not bad people; they were not mean or abusive, but neither did they care. They did not know Thomas or Gracie, nor did they ask the reason why Thomas and Gracie had to be placed into the foster child system.

When Thomas would cry at night in his bed, his foster mom would come in and say, "Try to get some sleep, Thomas. Everything gets better in time." Then she would pat Thomas on the back in an attempt to comfort him and walk out of the room.

Thomas continued going to school, enduring the torment from the other students and gleaning very small bits of information from his teachers. Gracie was placed into state-paid full-time daycare, and Thomas rarely saw her. He once asked his foster parents if they could take him to the church so he could see Abby and her family, but the foster parents said they were not allowed to foster religious influence. Twice Thomas walked the six miles to church, but Abby and her family had been out of town on those weekends. He even waited around after the services to speak with Pastor Phil, but the congregation usually mobbed the pastor, and Thomas didn't have the heart to speak out amongst the crowd.

After a year of daily pain and nightly tears, Thomas had forgotten all about his alleged trip to the Rio Vida. His mind dropped the memories like a heavy weight that could not be carried on a long journey. He did not think about the rope, the Santa Fe under the river, and the conflict with Jangk Stainkins. He didn't remember how Ken seemed to know about the river, talking about life's problems as if they were storms on the river; nor did he think about Spanish class where he learned that Rio Vida meant river of life and that Santa Fe meant holy faith. He repressed his memories of the fact that Jangk Stainkins really owned and operated the service station that Thomas had always feared. None of these memories had any power over the daily drip of uneventful boredom and pain. It was as if Thomas were on a long car trip and all those events were a town he passed through long ago; and now, after seeing a barren landscape for many miles, Thomas had forgotten all about the town and believed that only the barren landscape existed.

He thought about Abby and her family and how they seemed to be the long lost family he never had. But Thomas felt betrayed by them; they had not contacted him—not once. Thomas didn't know that Abby and her father had attempted many times to get the child protection officials to tell them Thomas's address, but the officials stood by their policy of not giving any information for the protection of the children and the foster families. Abby even tried going to Thomas's school to wait for him as he came out of class, but somehow they always missed each other. Eventually Abby believed that Thomas's foster parents must have moved him to another school.

Either way, Thomas did not know this information and believed he had been forgotten once again.

At school, Thomas wandered though the halls like a ghost without a place to haunt. He would bump into the occasional passing person. Most people just shoved him off; some who recognized Thomas made comments about the rumors they heard, calling him names like *freak* and *retard loser boy*. Usually Thomas didn't react, and sometimes he actually liked the attention; it was almost worse when the kids stared blankly showing Thomas he was not worth a reaction. *Bonk*—he just bumped into someone else.

"Frank," Thomas said faintly as he looked into Frank's face. Thomas had not spoken to Frank since that day in the lunchroom before Thomas's coma—before Thomas's mother died. He had seen Frank around school, but Frank never approached him. When Thomas returned to school after his time in the hospital, he wanted to tell Frank that he knew more about the group of planes that disappeared off the coast of Florida. He had not thought of it recently until just now. Looking into Frank's eyes, Thomas felt a tiny spark that would ignite everything he had vowed not to speak of. Thomas thought that Frank had a duty to be friendly, and Thomas craved friendliness. He wanted Frank to say, "Oh, hey, Thomas." This would show Thomas some personal connection, making a bridge Thomas could walk across and find comfort.

"Frank, you know this freaky kid?" said a boy walking with Frank.

"Um, he used to go to my church," Frank said as he looked back and forth between Thomas and the boy, "but I never hung out with him. I don't even remember his name."

Thomas snapped. He no longer had any reason to control himself. He had no one in his life to upset—no one whose opinion of him he cared about. Everyone in his life he cared about had left him and betrayed him. Thomas realized that nothing held him back from doing whatever he felt like doing.

"The name is Thomas, you preppy jerk," Thomas said as he thrust both hands toward Frank's chest, impacting Frank and sending him flying across the hallway, causing Frank's head to hit the wall. Everyone gathered around the two boys. Thomas felt the rush of adrenalin pump throughout his body. He remembered the feeling from his last fight with Sketch, but this time he felt he controlled the fight. This time the blood would not be Thomas's. He walked over to where Frank stood, stunned.

"Do you remember my name now, Frank-tard?" Thomas asked aggressively, but he did not wait for an answer. Thomas swung again at Frank, hitting him in the nose, causing a waterfall of blood to flow onto Frank's white shirt.

"Why did you do that?" Frank cried, trying not to inhale the blood flowing over his lips.

But there was no answer. Two teachers jumped into the crowd, grabbing both boys, and hauled them into the office. The principal wanted to suspend Thomas, but after looking at his grades, she decided that he just might like a day off. After Frank saw the school nurse, she sent them both back to class. The rest of the day passed uneventfully.

As Thomas walked home after school, three boys approached him.

"Good work today, man," said the first boy, who was named Bill. Bill had been known as a rough kid. He was not very strong or muscular looking, but his reputation generated fear in those around him. Just like Thomas, Bill had rumors told about him. Thomas heard that Bill had a probation officer keeping tabs on him because of something Bill had done involving a knife.

"What do you mean?" Thomas asked as he walked, looking straight ahead so as not to make eye contact with Bill.

"The way you just plugged that church-idiot right in the face," Bill said with excitement. The two other boys with Bill hollered in agreement. "Yeah, what did you call him? Frank-tard." The boys laughed in unison.

"Look, I don't know what happened. I just got mad at him and well … I don't know." Thomas had nothing to say.

"No, no. You don't have to say anything, dude," Bill said as he grabbed Thomas by the shoulder, turned him around, and looked him in the face. Thomas saw that the boys smiled at him. This disarmed Thomas, and he released a small smile in return. "Let me tell you, dude, you don't have to have a reason," Bill continued. "You just know that someone gets in your way, and you make him regret it. People won't give you what you want unless you take it from them."

"I really didn't want to hurt him … at first, I just felt angry when he pretended he didn't know who I was," Thomas explained candidly.

"So he disrespected you, and you made him respect you. Dude, that's how you live life," Bill said in a preacher's tone. "Your name's Thomas, right?" he asked, looking Thomas in the eye.

"Yeah, I'm Thomas."

"We have heard lots of stories about you," said Bill.

"Oh, great," said Thomas, rolling his eyes.

"No, no don't get me wrong, dude, I'm trying to tell you we don't care what other people say about you. You see, we all here have a lot of things said about us, you know, but when we hear something we don't like, we make that person respect us. Just like you did today," Bill looked at Thomas with a gleam in his eye Thomas had never seen before. Bill's lips were straight, but he seemed content.

His head tilted up, and his eyes contacted Thomas's. What Thomas didn't know was that this look was respect.

"What about guys that are bigger than you, you know … like that Sketchelmanger guy?" Thomas ashamedly inquired, not wanting to tear down his newfound fame.

"Oh yeah, we saw you in that fight," Bill said. "That guy was pretty big, but big guys usually are big chickens when they think they'll get hurt," Bill said as he patted his front pocket with his hand. Thomas nodded and smiled even though he didn't understand what Bill meant; Thomas liked his new friend's attention and did not want to demonstrate ignorance. "Look, Tom—that's what we'll call you—let's go hang out at our place."

The last time Thomas felt connected to some one was with Sal on the river, but that was not real to Thomas anymore; that was a dream. Bill and these new guys were real. Thomas agreed to hang out with his new friends. They walked out to a dirt field behind some buildings and out to a group of trees that formed a canopy. Inside the trees was a room about fifteen feet by fifteen feet; the floor had been dug out about a foot and was covered with carpet. Thomas saw empty soda and beer cans scattered all over the ground as well as the occasional adult magazine. Thomas at first felt ashamed of these items, but he reminded himself that no one cared about what he did anymore and that he shouldn't either. A charge of power and control surrounded Thomas as he joined in his new friends' activities. He felt like the king of his life and that no other cause but his royal desires had value; if no one else cared about his life, then he would.

"Hey Bill, we could use some juice, you catch me, man?" yelled one of the boys in the tree-covered room.

"I've been thinking about that," Bill said with a smirk. "Hey Tom, you ready to prove yourself?"

"Prove what?" Thomas asked without understanding.

"We here are a bit thirsty and are going to need a little refreshment. I was hoping you could, you know, help us out." Bill looked at Thomas, testing his perception.

"I'm sorry. I don't have any money," Thomas said regretfully.

"Money's not the problem. We just need someone to go pick up our refreshment for us at the quick mart on the corner."

"You mean the store gives you water for free?" Thomas asked innocently.

"Tom, dude," Bill said, frustrated at Thomas's cluelessness. "Beer, man. Go swipe us some beer."

"I can't steal," Thomas protested.

"It's not stealing," Bill reasoned. "Remember what we talked about earlier? About taking respect from those that don't give it? This is the same thing." Bill said this with such confidence that it commanded Thomas's respect and allegiance.

"I don't understand," Thomas said. "Are they just going to give it to us?"

"Tom, bro, you just walk in the store, go to the back and grab a few big bottles, put them in your pants, and walk the heck out. Dude, they don't know they owe it to us, but they do. You just take what they owe us ... right?" Bill spoke so militantly that it motivated Thomas to act and not question Bill. Thomas felt he had no right to protest the logic of those who had accepted him as a friend.

"All right." Thomas said as he nodded his head, biting his lower lip. "Let's do it." As he walked out of the tree-covered room, he saw a skeleton head someone had hung from one of the branches. For the first time since before his mother's death, Thomas thought of Jangk Stainkins and shuddered.

Thomas followed the group to the rear of the corner store and huddled to make the play.

"Just go in there like you own the place, Tom. Put the beer in your pants and get out of there," Bill said with the enthusiasm of a motivational speaker.

"Okay, here I go," Thomas said out loud, as if he had to confirm his actions. No one protested, and he went in.

Ding ding went the electronic bell as Thomas entered the store. Thomas saw two adults who looked too old to be working behind the counter. He saw a man in a white shirt and a blue tie walk back toward the beer cooler. At first the man seemed to notice Thomas, so Thomas ducked into the candy aisle where he felt he should logically be. He grabbed pieces of candy and pretended to care about the ingredients on each piece. He even made faces as to show concern over the horrible contents of each piece of candy to establish credibility with those who might be watching. A moment later, Thomas ducked around the corner and saw nobody else in the beer aisle. This was his chance; he went to the glass door that guarded the bottled beer, opened it, and grabbed two bottles, enough to satisfy everybody waiting outside. He shoved the bottles into his pants, causing his crotch to hurt from the cold, and limped out of the aisle like a kid who got kicked in the groin.

"Hey, kid. Stop!" yelled the excessively old person working behind the counter. Thomas ran toward the door, thinking that the person behind the counter could not catch him. He did not notice the other worker in the aisle. Thomas felt a hairy set of arms cover his face, taking Thomas to the ground and breaking the two bottles inside of his pants. Thomas instinctively threw his fist toward the man that had tackled him to the ground. He merely wanted to get away; it didn't occur to Thomas that he was being taken down because he was doing something criminal. With the side of his face pinned on the ground, Thomas saw his new friends running away.

CHAPTER 15

YELLOW SHIRT

THE WHITE PRISONER van waited for the big, black, iron gates to open. As the van slowly drove through the entryway, Thomas looked up and saw black letters on the archway: *"Juvenile Department of Corrections."* The judge gave Thomas two years to be corrected. That was an unusually long sentence for a juvenile theft, but the judge said when Thomas threw his hands toward the clerk, it made the theft a robbery. A theft means someone merely steals something, but it becomes robbery when force is combined with theft. This turns a small misdemeanor into a serious felony. Thomas tried to convince the judge that he only threw his arms toward the man because he thought the man meant him harm. The judge, however, had become callous from multiple juveniles who performed remorse in court only to be rearrested days later for another offence. This time the judge decided to hit heavy on the first offence.

Crack, echoed the solid metal door as the guard inside the control room opened it electronically. Thomas thought it was strange that there were no iron bars and guards using skeleton keys like on TV. Once inside, the smell of moldy, stale body odor plugged itself into Thomas's nostrils like two fingers; it reminded Thomas of school.

"Step in that cell, and strip to your underwear," said a man dressed in blue jeans and a polo shirt. The man stood only a few inches taller than Thomas and appeared to be only a few years older.

"To my underwear?" questioned Thomas. Immediately he thought of Chuck and began to feel nervous.

"Hurry kid!" grunted the short guard in control.

Thomas reluctantly pulled his pants down and took off his shirt. Thomas could not clearly recall his path to jail. Nothing was clear. It seamed his life kept revolving in the same pattern. He always wound up in a place where he did not ask to be put—places where he was forced to live by other people's rules without any guidance.

"Put this on," shouted the guard as he threw a yellow T-shirt and blue cloth pants at Thomas.

"Why is the shirt yellow?" Thomas asked as he pulled it over his head.

"Don't ask questions right now," snapped the short, boyish guard. "Just get dressed and follow me."

Thomas finished putting on his new clothes and walked to the edge of the entry cell.

"Okay, com'on," said the guard as he led Thomas to the main square of the building. The room had a desk in the middle where one guard sat and observed the sixteen little rooms with thick glass doors that housed other detained juveniles. Each door had something written on it with a white dry-erase marker.

"What is this room?" Thomas asked in a soft voice so the short guard would not feel threatened.

"This is the transfer room," he answered. "Anyone coming to the jail, like you, or anyone going out for trial or release comes through here." Thomas looked around the room and read the writing on each door. One door said "sentenced," another said "to trial." One girl had "runaway" written on her door with "parents contacted twenty-two hours," written underneath.

"Graves," called another guard holding a clipboard.

Not used to hearing his last name, Thomas didn't respond at first. "Oh, that's me. My name is Thomas," he finally said.

"Whatever," mumbled the guard. "Go in this cell."

Thomas stepped in, and the guard shut the solid glass door. The guard then took out his white marker and wrote on Thomas's door, "Sentenced, full term." Thomas stared at the white writing, wondering exactly what it meant. He tapped on the glass door until he got the guard's attention.

"Are you dying?" asked the guard gruffly as he slid the door open so rapidly that Thomas fell to the ground. Shocked. Thomas looked up at the guard with a face seeking an apology or some sympathy.

"Well, are you dying?" repeated the guard, pausing after every word for emphasis.

Thomas realized he would receive no sympathy. "No," he said softly, "I'm not dying."

"Then why on earth are you tapping with your dirty hand on my door?"

"I'm sorry," Thomas said in his best nonconfrontational voice. "I just wanted to know what sentenced means. I saw the kid across the room has the same word on his door."

Thomas pointed at a kid in another cell. The kid stood taller than Thomas by almost six inches and had the muscles of a strong man. He had dark hair, and from about thirty feet away, Thomas could see he also had dark eyes. "Did he steal beer like me?"

"Steal beer?" the guard said between gasps of laughter. "That kid is here for murder."

Thomas's senses failed him. His hearing stopped, his vision blurred, and his body went numb. It didn't seem possible to him that his actions could put him in the same place as murderers. He felt he needed to make an immediate appeal to the guard. "This must be a mistake, guard. I—"

"Guard?" said the guard angrily. "Kid you don't get it, do you? You better learn some respect. Here every guard is your daddy, and you will call us sir until you're told otherwise."

"I'm sorry ... Sir. It's just that there has to be a mistake."

"A mistake?" said the guard sarcastically. "Please tell me about the mistake. I would love to hear it."

"Yes ... Sir ... yes, there has been a mistake. I just stole some beer, and it wasn't even for me."

"Of course it wasn't," the guard confirmed with more sarcasm.

"No. I just tried to make my new friends happy. That can't be punished in the same way murder is punished ... right?"

The guard stared at Thomas, hoping that Thomas would regurgitate his own words and taste the lack of logic. Thomas stood oblivious. "Kid, you're in jail, and so is that kid over there who murdered. We didn't drive around in a van and snatch kids up who were minding their own business. You committed a crime. Therefore you are a criminal, and this is where criminals go when they get caught."

Thomas understood he could not convince the guard of the mistake. He felt as frustrated as he did when he tried to convince his mother of his dream. Thomas accepted that no adults believed him; eventually Thomas did not even believe it himself. Thomas dropped all protest. "Well," he began, "what is that kid's name?"

The guard stared at Thomas, wondering why Thomas cared about the murderer's name. "The name's Hector," he said. "Don't make him mad. If you do, you might never leave." The guard then shut the glass door roughly, locked it, and walked away. Thomas laid down on the concrete bench and eventually fell asleep. *Bang, bang …* Thomas woke to the sound of a different guard pounding on the door.

"Graves," said the guard boomingly, opening the glass door. Thomas stared at the guard with sleepy eyes.

"Are you Graves or not?" the guard repeated.

"Yes. I'm Thomas. That's me," Thomas said, still half-asleep.

"All right," said the guard. "Let's go."

"Where are we going?" asked Thomas, trying to wake up.

"We're going to your main quarters," said the guard. "I see you came in with a yellow shirt. That's good."

"Why? What difference does that make?" Thomas asked.

"Yellow means neutral, neither good nor bad; almost like a fresh start, you know, morning. If you get a green shirt, it means you're in good favor with the department—like you have behaved well and done a good job showing that you have been … well … corrected."

Thomas remembered that Hector, the kid in for murder, had on a red shirt. Walking away, he glanced over to Hector's glass cell; it was empty.

"What does the red shirt mean?" asked Thomas.

"Yeah, the red shirt," said the guard, smirking. "That means that your behavior has not been exactly above reproach."

"Oh, you mean like if you did something bad to get in here, like murder?"

"No," said the guard. "It doesn't matter what you did to get in here, it's all how you behaved once you've gotten here."

"So the murderer kid, Hector, did something bad after he got here?" Thomas questioned.

"Yeah, something like that. Must have been pretty bad to get a red shirt in the ten minutes it takes to come from intake."

As Thomas and the guard walked down the hallway, Thomas saw that the windows were dark, indicating that it was nighttime.

"We're going to your quarters now," continued the guard. "If you play your cards right, you get yourself a green shirt."

"That's good, right?" questioned Thomas.

"Well … means you have shown yourself to be responsible. But don't go getting a green shirt right away."

"Why not?"

"The other kids will think you're a brown noser, and you don't want that said of yourself here."

"Oh," said Thomas. He wasn't sure what a brown noser was. He recalled that in school the kid who reminded the teacher to give homework was called a brown noser. Thomas figured since there was no homework in jail, he would not have to worry about it.

The guard held up an ID badge to a security pad that opened the double doors before them. They walked outside and passed through a chain-link fence tunnel covered with razor wire.

"I'll bet no one ever tried to break out of here," Thomas commented.

"Oh, you'll be surprised. Many have tried, and a few have succeeded."

"Don't they get bloody from all that wire?" Thomas asked, shocked that anyone would try such a thing.

"Of course they do."

"But why would anyone want to do that? Is this place that bad?"

"This place is no different than anywhere else," the guard said. "It will be what you make it. It's when the kids lose hope that they do all types of stupid things. It's no different than the world outside, right? If you don't have hope or faith in something, life becomes meaningless."

"Yeah, I guess that makes sense," Thomas said as he remembered all he had gone through in life. He thought about the river and the rope, the Santa Fe. "The holy faith," Thomas muttered, thinking about how the rope saved him in his dream.

"What did you mumble?" asked the guard.

"Nothing," Thomas quickly said. He did not want to be deceived by his feelings telling him that his river dream might be true. He thought he had dismissed that fantasy long ago, but something inside of Thomas would not allow him to dismiss the feeling completely. "What's that sound?" Thomas asked, hearing running water.

"That's the pool," said the guard. "Oh, you'll love the pool."

"Really, we can swim here?"

"No, kid, you can't. Some genius in the state legislature thought that all the kids here needed to be corrected with an Olympic-sized swimming pool. She thought that maybe having Olympic aspirations would give kids the hope we just spoke of."

"So why can't we swim?" Thomas asked.

"Because kids in a correctional facility don't just develop Olympic aspirations. They instead use the pool as a giant toilet. They did this so many times that it broke the filters, and now it's too dirty to swim in. The water you hear is the water that sprays just under the diving board to mark the landing point. The valve to turn it off got rusted in the open position."

"Why don't they just drain the pool?"

"Can't. They built the pool without checking the federal regulations. They need to redo the pipes to have the federally approved drainage system for an Olympic-sized pool. But to redo the pipes costs about a million dollars in order to drain a half million dollar pool."

"Isn't it dangerous to have a big, dirty pool around a bunch of wild kids?"

"I agree, but the bosses are more afraid of government regulations. Besides, dead kids are better publicity to get more government money."

"Has anyone ever drowned here?" Thomas asked nervously.

"Almost—it's funny you ask that," the guard said amused. "When they installed the pool, they placed these ropes at the bottom."

"Ropes?" Thomas repeated as he turned his head toward the guard.

"Yeah, ropes," the guard said. "They were put in because they figured the kids here might not be able to swim well. So if they started to drown, the kid could go to the bottom and pull the rope."

"What good would that do?"

"When rope is pulled, it's supposed to turn on a red light and drain the pool. The rope is like a lifeline."

The image was eerily similar to his dream. He could not dismiss an underwater rope designed to save people's lives as a coincidence. He fought the feeling that the river dream was true.

"So, no kid here ever pulled the rope as a prank?" Thomas asked.

"The pool was designed for a high dive, so it's about twenty-five feet deep. Most of the kids here can't swim well and were too scared to go that far under water."

They came to another set of double doors. The guard lifted his ID card to the security pad, and the doors opened.

"You'll get a bunk mate here," the guard said as they walked into the room. "Everyone shares a room. Don't expect him to like you right away. Nobody likes anyone here until they can trust him."

Thomas looked around the room and saw kids looking as young as eight and as old as twenty-five all with yellow, green, and red shirts. The moment Thomas walked in, they all stopped whatever they were doing and stared at Thomas.

"Fresh meat," someone yelled, but the guard belted out a firm, "Knock it off," preventing any other comments. Thomas kept his head down, not wanting to look anyone else in the eyes. Thomas and the guard passed, and the kids went back to their activities.

"Right here, kid; this room is yours," the guard said, pointing inside a dark, cave-like hole. Thomas could see a metal, creaky bunk bed and a person in a red shirt on the bottom bunk.

"What do I do now?" asked Thomas. "Just go in?"

"You can do what you want until lights out time. That happens at ten. Good luck, kid."

The guard left, and Thomas was left standing in the dark room with a red-shirted kid who appeared to be asleep. Thomas felt like he was in a cave with a sleeping dragon. Thomas lightly walked over to the edge of the bed and grabbed onto the top railing in order to hoist himself up. He did this softly so as to not wake up the red shirt. *Creeeeak* went the bed as Thomas pulled his body toward the top bunk. He paused to assess the situation. The red shirt had not moved, so Thomas again pulled himself toward the top of the bunk, confident that the red shirt still slept.

"These beds are way too noisy," said a voice from below. Thomas froze with a bone-chilling stiffness. He had not felt this intensely afraid since he saw Jangk Stainkins on the river. Thomas remembered with Stainkins he had to face his fear, and he knew he had to do the same now. Thomas slowly lowered himself so he could see the red shirt on the bottom bunk. It was Hector—the murderer.

CHAPTER 16

THE MURDERER

THOMAS DID NOT move or speak. He felt like a deer in the headlights of an oncoming vehicle. He stared at Hector noticing, his dark features, the olive-colored skin and dark hair. He thought Hector's dark features with the red shirt made him appear like a black widow spider. Up close, Thomas noticed that Hector had light blue eyes that emitted brightness, contrasting his dark features.

"Dude, can you talk?" asked Hector with a concerned voice. This eased Thomas's fears, prompting him to speak.

"Ye … yes. I can talk. I'm sorry I woke you. I was just trying to get to my bunk so I could sleep too."

"I wasn't sleeping." Hector said.

"I'm sorry," Thomas returned. "I thought you were asleep."

"You say sorry for everything, don't you?" Hector stated.

"I'm sorry," Thomas said again and then closed his eyes, wishing he could erase what he just said. "I guess you're right. I'm just very nervous being here. You know, like it's a mistake that I'm here."

"A mistake that you're here? Or you're here because you made a mistake?"

Thomas perceived that Hector was smarter than he thought. "Wow, I guess—"

"No, it's not a question to be answered," Hector said curtly. "I have been thinking about it myself. That's why I can't sleep."

As Hector finished his sentence, a fight broke out in the other room. Thomas heard all forms of insults and vulgarities, each one about the other kid's mother.

"You hear that?" Hector asked as he motioned toward the ruckus. "I'm not like those boys out there. They have no respect for life or for themselves." Just then, two guards walked slowly past the room on their way to the brawl. They were in no hurry. Hector stood out of his bed, reaching his full height of six feet, two inches. Thomas already had a fearful respect for Hector because of the murder charge and the red shirt. Now he feared him for his size and intelligence too. This intimidated Thomas from asking the question he really wanted to ask. Thomas could hear the guards breaking up the fight in the background.

"Look, man, sorry. I don't even know you name," Hector said.

"I'm Thomas."

"All right, Thomas. Looks like we're going to have to figure this stuff out together. By the way I'm—"

"I know. Your name is Hector."

"What!" Hector shouted. Thomas stiffened up and took a step backward. He felt like he had stepped on a mine in a battlefield. "Where did you get that name!" Hector shouted.

Thomas noticed the guards coming toward their cell. They opened the door. "Hey, red shirt, what's your problem? You can't afford any negative attention or you're going solitary."

"It was me," Thomas exclaimed quickly. "It's my fault."

"That wasn't you, you little liar," the guard yelled. "Your voice is like an angry cat, and his is like a mama bear. I know I didn't hear any cats."

"I know," said Thomas quickly, "but I was trying to get to my bunk and I stepped on his face. He just reacted. It's not his fault."

The guards looked at each other and then back at Thomas. "Okay, kitty," the one guard said. "Don't do too many stupid things on your first day. And as for you, red shirt, watch yourself." The guards left the room.

"Look," said Hector, "I wasn't upset at you, and although that was awesome that you covered for me, don't lie to them. They will make life hard for you if they think you're a liar."

"What were you mad at then?" Thomas asked, sensing a small bond forming.

"That name, Hector. Where did you get that?" Hector asked calmly.

"The first guard at the intake told me that was your name," Thomas said.

"Exactly, I knew it. You see, Thomas, that guard is the reason for my red shirt."

"I don't understand," said Thomas.

"My name is Mathew, or Matt I guess is what everybody calls me. But that jerk called me Hector just because I look Mexican."

"Aren't you Mexican?" asked Thomas cautiously.

"Yes, I am and proud of it, but that's not the point. In the intake cell he asked me my name, and I said Mathew. Then he tells me that there is no way I could look as Mexican as I do and not have a Mexican name. I told him all calm and polite that my name was Mathew. He then tells me, 'Well, I'm calling you Hector,' so I got angry with him and shoved him. I knew I shouldn't have done it, but I hurt so badly at that moment. I mean, I just got sentenced, and I wanted someone I could talk with or a least just be left alone. I didn't need that fool giving me such crap."

"Sorry … Mathew or Matt. I didn't know."

"I know you didn't, man. Like I said, I wasn't mad at you," Matt said. "So I guess then he told you what I'm in for."

"Yeah," said Thomas lightly, not wanting to step on another mine. "He did. You don't have to tell me anything about it."

"No, that's just it. I have to talk about it. Just like I asked earlier, is it a mistake that I'm here or am I here for a mistake?"

"But you killed someone. That's not a mistake, was it?" Thomas asked, realizing he may have overstepped his bounds with his new roommate.

"I know what it sounds like, Thomas, but think about it. It really is only a few seconds that put me here. If I had killed the loser three seconds earlier, I would not be here."

"I really don't understand," Thomas said, confused.

"Look, my mom married this jerk named Candalario."

"Candalario?" asked Thomas. "That sounds like one of those expensive perfumes they sell in the big stores at the mall."

Matt laughed hard for a few seconds. "I wish he could have heard that one. But really, he was bad. He would come over after work and drink all night and yell at my mother. It kept getting worse and worse. The cops would come all the time, and my mother would always lie to them and tell them that she started the fight and that it was just verbal arguing.

"One night I came home late from soccer practice, and I walked in on him beating her. I mean he was waling on her face to the point that I thought she was dead. I don't know why, but I froze. You know how you always picture yourself being a great hero when you think about these things, and you think you will jump in just in time to help someone? It's not like that. I just froze. He turned around, saw me, and then stopped. He started to walk away while looking at me, and that's when it finally kicked in. I grabbed him, threw him on the ground, and punched him in the face until he stopped moving."

"That was like in defense of your mom, right?" Thomas asked.

"No, three seconds. That's what I meant. If I killed him three seconds earlier, it would have been in defense of my mom." Matt drifted off into thought, and Thomas found himself becoming fond of the murderer who had terrified him a few moments earlier.

"What did your real father think?" Thomas asked.

"My real father?" Matt asked, waking from his thoughts. "I never knew him. He left my mother before I was born. I hope he rots."

Another fight broke out in the main hall, and again the guards slowly walked toward the tussle. "Everyone down," they shouted. "On the count of three, everyone not on the ground face down will get a bean bag in their back."

"Let's get down, Thomas," Matt ejected.

"We're not part of the fight, though," said Thomas in protest.

"Just do it. I'm sure they're just looking for a chance to bag anyone they can." Thomas and Matt got down on the ground. "Man, I tell you I'm not like these other kids," he said as they lay face down on the ground. "I wish someone would throw me a lifeline. I would leave here as soon as I could."

"A lifeline?" Thomas asked. "Do you mean like a rope?"

"Sure, a rope, whatever. Anything that can get me out of here. At least that feeling that someone or something can see my heart and not just my crime."

The guards came in the cell and yelled, "One at time, state your name."

"Thomas Graves," said Thomas.

"And you, red shirt?" the guards yelled.

"My name," Matt paused. Thomas hoped that Matt would cooperate and give his name without getting upset. "My name is Mathew Gonzalez," Matt said slowly, as if he wanted to say something else but held it back.

"All right, lights out. Let's go, everybody," shouted the guards. The lights came off in the main room, and other kids went into their rooms. The lights shut off in all the cells. Only a small sliver of moonlight came through the five-inch crack of a window with six-inch safety glass.

Thomas remembered his apartment bedroom where he stayed with his mother and how the moonlight came through the crack in the blinds. He grew sick in the belly thinking about that time in his life. If he had listened in English class, Thomas would have known he was feeling melancholy. He missed his mother and Gracie. He wondered about Gracie. He figured she would be about five now and wondered if she thought of him.

He felt drowsy but could not fall asleep. The river dream still nagged him. The guard's talk of hope and faith being essential for one's survival in jail, the swimming pool with life saving ropes at the bottom, and Matt's desiring a lifeline or rope could not all have been coincidences. But Thomas had learned to hate the dream. What good had it ever brought? Since the dream, Thomas's mother had died, Abby's family had abandoned him, and now he was lying on a cold bunk in jail. He felt the dream was as useless as Sal, who spoke mysteriously, never giving solid answers; thinking of the river made Thomas feel hot in the face, as if fire burned his skin down to the skull.

CHAPTER 17

HANDS ON FIRE

BANG, BANG ... THE guards pounded every cell with their fists, shouting, "Everybody up, roll call in five minutes." Thomas heard the bang and felt that he must have fallen asleep only moments before. All night long his thoughts prevented his rest. He looked over at Matt's bunk and saw that he still slept.

"Wake up, man," he said as he shook Matt lightly.

"Stop," yelled Matt, as he violently reached over and seized Thomas's arm. "Dad, I told you—" He then sat up, looking into Thomas's eyes with his own wild, fire eyes. "Thomas," he said, startled, as his eyes returned to a cool blue. "I'm sorry. I forgot where I was."

"That's okay," said Thomas cautiously. "Could you let go of my arm though?"

"Yeah, sorry again."

Thomas rubbed his arm with his hand as he backed away from Matt and walked toward the door. Matt got up, and they walked down the hall together to the main room.

"Line up in colors," shouted the guard. Thomas watched as the red shirts, including Matt, tried to form a single line that looked more like the paper wrapper taken off a drinking straw.

"Seriously ladies," shouted the guard, "cover down!" The line got slightly straighter but not much. Thomas realized he needed to get himself in line with the yellow shirts. He placed himself behind another yellow shirt, forming a line more crooked than the red shirts'.

"Yellow shirts!" yelled the guard, who was about to say something else when a tiny voice interrupted him.

"That's okay, guard," said a voice so soft that Thomas thought it was a woman's. "Yellow shirts, remember your circle of respect," said the same soft voice. Thomas didn't know what a circle of respect was, so he stood in place, hoping for an explanation. No one else seemed to be doing anything differently; all the other kids talked among themselves, and some began shouting. "Respect boys, respect," said the soft voice without any result.

"Where's that voice coming from?" Thomas asked the yellow shirt behind him.

"That's the director," said the boy.

"They let a woman be in charge of a boy's jail?" Thomas asked. The boy rolled his eyes at Thomas, indicating that Thomas needed to shut his mouth.

"You're an idiot," mumbled the boy as Thomas turned back around.

"Yes, son, I am very much a man."

Thomas turned around and saw a thin man about forty years old standing at five foot, nine inches. He stood hunched over, with his hands behind his back; if he stood straight up, he would have been six-foot even. His eyes and hair were brown, and he dressed himself in a pair of khaki pants and a white polo shirt. "I speak softly, son, because I'm trying to speak directly to your humanity."

Thomas did not understand what that meant. He felt more pity for the director then fear. "You may call me Sam, son," the director said as he reached out, touching Thomas's shoulder.

"Sam … sir?" asked Thomas, unsure of why the director of the prison wanted to be addressed by his first name.

"No, not Sir. Call me Sam," the director softly reaffirmed. The other boys became restless and fought with each other so loudly that no one could hear anything anyone was saying.

"Oh, for all things holy," mumbled the main guard under his breath. Then he puffed out his broad chest, clinched his fists, and yelled at the top of his lungs, "Everybody line up straight, line up now, or everybody loses outside time for a whole week!" Immediately the boys snapped into five perfect columns without a sound.

"Thank you, guard," said Director Sam as he stared into the guard's eyes with controlled anger. "I want to begin the day with a reminder to respect those around you by first respecting yourself." The boys lightly murmured at the remark.

"Respect my …" an unknown boy mumbled, but a firm *"ahem"* from the main guard clearing his throat returned the boys to silence. Director Sam made a few more remarks but nothing important.

The rest of the day consisted of various fights among the boys and guards breaking up those fights. In between the fights teachers were brought in to attempt education, but the only subject that brought the boys together was a comparison of their fathers' prison sentences. But that too produced fights when one boy thought his father's crime and sentence topped another boy's father.

After a few days, Thomas learned to not speak to anyone; this kept him under the radar of the other boys and the guards. Thomas tried to talk to Matt in the main room, but he learned quickly that different-colored shirts didn't mingle in front of the guards. Matt would tell Thomas not to talk to him so Thomas would not be labeled as a red shirt wannabe.

Thomas looked forward to nighttime when he could speak with Matt in their cell. Matt told Thomas about his childhood when his stepfather married his mother and how he would come home drunk and get into fistfights with Matt. This ironically comforted Thomas, who felt if he did have a father, he might have been violent like Matt's.

After weeks inside the boys' prison, Thomas forgot about the coincidences that reminded him of the river. Matt never again talked about a lifeline, and Thomas forgot about the swimming pool with its ropes. Without realizing it, Thomas slowly slipped into the faithless, hopeless drone the guard had warned him about. When Matt would ask Thomas about his family, Thomas would say, "I never had a family. They all left me." Soon Thomas began fighting like all the other kids without regard for others or himself. Thomas went into boys' prison for a simple theft, but he learned to deal with life like a serious felon. His anger burned his flesh like fire—fire that burned down to the skull.

One morning after another reckless roll call, Thomas noticed a new kid with a yellow shirt. Nothing special stuck out about this kid. Eventually Thomas learned his name was Earl and that he came from the same town as Thomas. Thomas felt a duty to initiate Earl into the prison with special attention. At night he told Matt about his plans to embarrass Earl at roll call the next morning, but Matt, the murderer, cautioned Thomas against the idea, stating that nobody deserves to be humiliated.

Thomas, however, did not agree. He felt that Earl had been too quiet, quieter than Thomas had been, and that he needed some special treatment to break his quiet shell. For an unexplained reason Thomas felt irritated that Earl came from the same town; it made Thomas feel he had to make Earl bitter like him. The next morning Thomas prepared to haze the rookie prisoner. Earl stood in front of

Thomas at roll call. Thomas reached down toward Earl's waistline. His plan was to yank Earl's pants and underwear to his knees. As Thomas reached down, his hands felt like they were on fire. He ignored it, thinking it was nervousness, but the burn increased, forcing him to stop and look down at his hands.

"Impossible," Thomas shrieked in fear, closing his eyes in disbelief.

That night in the room, Matt asked Thomas why the plan had failed.

"You wouldn't believe me if I told you, man," said Thomas, still somber from the experience.

"No really. I want to know," Matt countered. "I was angry at you earlier. I thought that you had become stupid like the rest of the kids here, but I'm very glad to see that I was right to think you were different. So tell me."

"I knew this guy once … or I guess I should say I kind of knew of this guy," Thomas fumbled his words. "Anyway, this guy had a bunch of bad things happen to him, and he couldn't handle it. So he tried to burn himself rather than deal with his problems."

"That's horrible," interjected Matt. "But I don't get what that has to do with you."

"Well, that's just it. He survived the burn … well, kind of."

"You saw him after?" Matt said, surprised and horrified.

"Yes, well I think I did." Thomas paused, thinking about how much he wanted to reveal. "Either way, much of his flesh was burned off, leaving only his bones with a few pieces of charred flesh. And when I reached down to grab Earl's pants, I felt a burning in my hands. So I looked at then and saw the same bony, burned hands I saw on this guy."

"Really?" Mat said, puzzled. "Like in a symbolic way?"

"No. I know it sounds crazy, but I actually saw the burned

hands, and I felt them too. They felt stiff, hot, and it smelled horrible. I have never smelled anything like it."

"Yeah, that does sound a bit crazy, but whatever. It kept you from doing evil to another person."

Thomas realized that Matt was right. What Thomas learned in the dream prevented him from harming another person as well as himself. Thomas recognized that just like Jangk Stainkins, Thomas had become bitter toward his life, and this bitterness had caused Thomas to desire harm to others and to himself.

"Whatever happened to that guy, Thomas?" Matt asked.

"I don't know, but I have a feeling I'm going to find out."

Thomas said no more. He felt relieved he had not pulled down Earl's pants, yet he hated that he had become so low. There was no excuse for it. Thomas had a clear example of the result of bitterness in Stainkins, but to acknowledge Jangk Stainkins as an example was to acknowledge that the river dream was valid. Thinking wore Thomas out, and he fell asleep doubting his ability to understand.

He mumbled his way to sleep: "God, if you're there, I still need victory."

CHAPTER 18

BREAD IN THE DESERT

BANG, BANG ... The guards pounded on each door to wake all the prisoners. Thomas rose to line up and hear Director Sam's speech about the healing power of respect. After the speech, Thomas walked over to the classroom to await the day's attempt at education.

"Thomas Graves," called the head guard on duty. "Report up front. You got a visitor."

"A visitor? Who is it?" Thomas asked, surprised.

"Kid, I don't know. Go find out." The guard escorted Thomas to the visitor room. The room did not have thick glass window separating two people who had to talk on phones like in the movies. It was an open room where the visitor could be close to the prisoner. The guard held up his ID badge to the security pad, letting himself and Thomas into the room. Thomas saw a man with dark hair sitting with his back to Thomas. He felt nervous not knowing who his visitor was. No one knew Thomas other than people in the criminal justice system. As Thomas approached, the man turned around and extended his arm toward Thomas.

"Thomas, it's great to see you." It was Ken, Abby's father. Thomas felt stunned, but he then reached out his own hand to meet Ken's.

He felt a swirl of emotions. The anger of abandonment came out first but was followed by the comfort of good memories.

"How did you know I was here?" Thomas asked squeakily, unsure of what tone to take.

"Thomas, I have been looking for you ever since you were placed in foster care," Ken said, grabbing Thomas's shoulders. Thomas stiffened his body in response to Ken's touch. "Thomas, you know that my mother became very sick and I had to bring her into our house to take care of her."

"Yeah, I remember," Thomas said coldly.

"I'm sorry, Thomas. I just couldn't support a sick mother, you, and your sister at the time," Ken said, leaving one arm on Thomas' shoulder.

"Do you know where Gracie is now?" asked Thomas, hoping it would slightly injure Ken's conscience.

"Yes, Thomas, I do. She lives with us," Ken said, returning his second arm to Thomas's shoulder and smiling. "We are in the process of adopting her."

Thomas dropped his stiff shoulders and stared into Ken's face. The bitterness from abandonment left Thomas. "How did you find her?" Thomas asked in amazement.

"I have a friend from work who has a sister who works for Child Protection Services."

"Does Gracie remember me?" asked Thomas with big, eager eyes.

"Of course she does. She says a prayer for you every night," Ken said, smiling.

"What about me? How did you know I was here?" Thomas asked.

"Child Protection Services does not have a record of you being arrested. The record merely states that you left the program." Ken looked at Thomas with a mild smirk, indicating the stupidity of the system. "So I have been searching for you ever since. Finally one day last week, I found your name on a county court website. I applied for the court transcripts from your case and found that you got sentenced here. So I came here hoping to find you. And well—"

"I'm sorry about all this, Ken. I'm sure you probably think less of me for this," Thomas said, putting his head down and looking at the ground.

"Well, you did steal a pretty cheap brand of beer …" Ken stopped and waited for Thomas to look up and see Ken's smile. "I would have gone for the big stuff myself." Thomas looked at Ken, amazed by his genuine smile. Thomas belted out a chuckle but stopped himself because he felt tears coming. He took a moment to compose himself.

"I thought you guys abandoned me," Thomas said, clearing his throat and then pausing to hold back more tears, "but you were seeking me the whole time. I feel so stupid for making the choices I did, and it was all based on what I thought you guys did, which wasn't true."

"Thomas," Ken said after a few moments, "I have to tell you something else."

Thomas felt curious but not nervous. There was nothing to be nervous about. Everyone in his family was gone except for Gracie, and she was safe.

"I know you made references a while ago to the comment I made about storms on the river of life." Thomas looked at Ken with intense eyes. "I remember Abby telling me some of the questions you asked her. Then I thought about what you were probably trying to ask me on that night we went to see your mom in the hospital."

Thomas now felt nervous. He had used all his energy in the past few years repressing and dismissing everything about his river dream. Now, in a twenty-four-hour period, he had seen himself as Jangk Stainkins and Ken had returned to talk about the river. "I believe I knew what you were talking about, but I was too scared to talk with you about it."

"What do you mean?" Thomas said in a whisper, barely able to believe his ears. "Have you been there?" he asked.

"No, but I believe my grandfather was."

"Did he tell you about it himself?" Thomas shot-gunned to Ken.

"No. I actually never met my grandfather. He died before I was born; actually, he died before my dad was born."

"I'm lost. I don't understand," said Thomas with a scrunched, puzzled face.

"Sometimes I'm not sure I do either," Ken said, taking a deep breath. "You see, my grandmother was pregnant with my father when my grandfather went to flight training during World War II. His name was Joseph, and he never actually fought in the war. He died in a training accident flying off of the coast of Florida."

Thomas was struck numb by what he heard. He remembered Ensign Joe from the river and what Joe said about the Santa Fe—the rope under the river.

"Ensign Joe," belted out Thomas.

"Yes he was an ensign in the navy, Thomas." Ken looked at Thomas with a stupefied look, as if Thomas had just shown Ken a three-headed monster. "How did you know that?"

"Just go on with your story first," Thomas said, not wanting to reveal too much.

"Well, he was killed in a training accident, like I said, before my father was born."

"Then how was he able to tell your father anything about the river?"

"This is where it gets a little weird," Ken said, rolling his eyes upward, as if he were seeking help.

"My father fought in the Vietnam War. He saw terrible things, and I believe him after hearing him scream in his sleep at times. Anyway, in Vietnam, he got shot and was brought to the medical tent. He says he was put under so the doctors could operate and try to get the bullet out and stop the bleeding. My father was a Christian man, like myself, and he prayed to God as they were about to operate on him. The next thing he knew, he was sitting in a room with another man who said he was his father. My dad said he didn't understand it, but he knew it to be true. Anyway this man—my grandfather—told my father that he could not give him all the answers to life, but that he would give him something that would help. That's when he told my father all about life being a river and how he needed to secure his raft so he could be stable in life."

"The raft," Thomas blurted out, unable to contain himself.

"Yes, a raft. He also told my father the raft was useless unless he tied himself down to the rope underneath the river. He said he had to have faith that the rope would save him during the storms on the river and after the waterfall."

"This is too much to take in," Thomas said, looking at Ken with large eyes. "I knew on the inside I wasn't wrong for believing I went to the river, but I sure felt crazy for it; I still do."

"Thomas, I have felt crazy since that night you started to speak of these things," Ken said, shaking his head. "I always thought my dad made up this story just to help us kids get through life."

"So did you know what I was talking about when I asked you about the river and storms that night in the hospital?" Thomas asked.

"I had a feeling you were referring to it, yes."

"Why didn't you talk about it with me?" asked Thomas with

a disappointed voice. "I would have been saved from years of grief and possibly might have avoided this place if I had known I was not such a freak."

Ken closed his eyes and flattened his smile. "Thomas, I have asked myself the same question. I'm sorry I let you down. I felt scared, nervous. You thought you were crazy! How do think I felt when this kid I never met before told me things that my father had told me long ago?"

"I guess you're right," Thomas conceded.

"Thomas, these days the church tells you to seek God. But if someone says they had a vision from God, the rest of the church thinks you're absolutely crazy. And they have good reason. Many people have claimed to have had a vision from God and then used that to start cults and control people. God doesn't give you dreams and visions so you can gain power over anyone else."

"I believe you're right, but then what is this all for?" Thomas asked while tears started to form in his eyes from much emotion.

"Well, I can't tell you what God wants from you. That's for you to find out from him. But that's why it he gave you your dream. So that you would find out more about him yourself."

"I don't see why God wants anything to do with my life. It seems he just keeps letting really bad things happen to me. Why would he want to give me this vision to know him better only to let horrible things happen to me?"

"I can't explain it because I don't know. But it seems to me that he may have given you the vision because he knew what events were going to happen to you. And he wanted you to have help."

"Look, I see what you're trying to say, but it seems a little ridiculous to me that God would make me go to this mystery place where everything is a riddle. Why doesn't he just come right out and say, 'Hey, I'm God, and this is exactly what I want you to do'? Why does it have to be this stupid mystery where bad things happen to good people and we have disease and war and only certain people get the right answer?" Thomas broke down in frustration and put his hands in his head.

"Thomas, I'm sorry," Ken said as he placed his hand on Thomas's shoulder. "The only thing I can think of is the story of Jesus being tempted in the desert."

Thomas looked up at Ken with a puzzled red face.

"You know, the story where Satan comes to Jesus after Jesus fasted for forty days in the desert."

"Yeah, I remember hearing the story," Thomas said with the same puzzled look.

"Satan tempted Jesus to come down from the top of the temple so the people would worship him. I never understood how that tempted Jesus. But I once heard a man say it was a popularly held belief in Jesus's day that the Messiah would ascend from the temple to let everyone know he was the Messiah."

"I see, but I still don't see how this relates," Thomas said.

"If Jesus wanted people to believe in Him as the Messiah, why would He not do what the people believed the Messiah should do? I mean, wouldn't that seem to solve the problem? The people would believe, and Jesus would be recognized as the Messiah."

"So what's the answer?" Thomas asked. "Why didn't he do what would have made him the Messiah in people's eyes?"

"Because he wants you to seek him for himself—for who he really is, not for who you want him to be. This relates to your vision and your question. God obviously let you see something of himself. But you have to seek out the meaning of it in your own life or else it will not be true to you; it will just be something someone else told you. That doesn't mean that God molds himself to you—no—but you have to mold your life to find God. And your vision is a piece of him he revealed to you. If God is not God to you in the context of your own life, then he will not be real."

"I think I see what you mean, but this is so much to take in. I have so many more questions," Thomas said with the same red, flushed face.

"Well, wouldn't this then be one of your storms?" Ken asked, smiling.

"That's it, time's up," said the guard.

"Thomas," said Ken, rising from his seat, "I will get in touch with you again, and I'm praying for you."

Thomas again broke into tears; no man had ever shown such interest in Thomas. As Ken walked toward the door, Thomas yelled out with an emotion-clogged voice, "Say hello to Abby for me."

"Yes, Abby," said Ken as the guard ushered him out. "I almost forgot. She went to college this year, said she met the guy she is going to marry. I'll tell her you said hi."

And the iron door slammed shut, leaving Thomas still a prisoner.

CHAPTER 19

BLOOD TRAIL

"MET THE MAN she is going to marry." Thomas played these words over and over in his head.

Thomas defined confusion; the God of the universe had personally tried to communicate to Thomas, but all he could think about was Abby in love with someone else. This clouded Thomas's mind, robbing him of clear thought. He had not spoken to Abby in a few years since his mother died, but he felt he had a connection with her. To Thomas she was beauty—not lust, beauty—which had given him the vision that something in life was worth living for. Logic shouted that God's vision was far more valuable than his feelings for Abby. Yet part of Thomas's spirit knew his feelings for Abby had been part of God's plan all along. Thomas realized he could do nothing about Abby; he had to let her go. Forced to let go of his mother, he now had to release Abby.

Thomas remembered the story of Abraham in the Bible. God asked Abraham to sacrifice his only son, and yet Abraham chose to believe God rather than human common sense. People have killed their kids, only to give the excuse that God told them to do it. This is what Ken must have meant when he said that many people consider visions from God to be insanity. After thinking, Thomas understood that the point of the story was not the sacrificing of children but the sacrificing of one's comforts to find God.

"The raft," Thomas said out loud while lying on his bunk.

"What did you mumble, Thomas?" asked Matt, sounding more somber than usual.

"Oh nothing, sorry," Thomas said, realizing he had spoken out loud. He then thought to himself, *I had to leave the comfort of the raft to find the rope below the water. The river was the Rio Vida, the river of life, and the rope was the Santa Fe, the holy faith. I had to leave the comforts of life to find true faith, which was not visible from the surface of life. Everything I love,* thought Thomas, *is on the surface of life: my mother, Abby, and Gracie. I have to leave them on the surface of life while I searched for true faith. I see, and once I'm connected to the true holy faith, I can handle the storms of life on the surface of the river.* Thomas thought further, *That's what Ken meant when he spoke of Jesus and the Temple. Is Jesus the rope? If so, that's the lifeline. I get it!*

"Hey Matt!" Thomas shouted. "I've got your lifeline!" But there was only silence. Matt had gone to sleep. "I'll tell him in morning," Thomas said quietly, realizing Matt was sleeping.

Thomas woke in the middle of the night and leaped off his bunk to get some water. He glanced at Matt's bunk; perhaps Matt was awake and could hear about the lifeline. But Thomas looked at an empty bunk. He looked around the room, finding no sign of Matt anywhere. Under the bunks, behind the dresser—nothing; Matt was gone. *Of course,* Thomas thought. *Matt probably went to the restroom.* Thomas waited for a half an hour before he checked the restroom himself. The restroom was out the door and down the hall. A guard stood in the hall at night to monitor the boys' movements, but when Thomas asked permission to use the restroom, he saw the guard was sleeping.

"Figures," Thomas said to himself, walking slowly to the restroom where he expected to find Matt. Thomas opened the door slowly and went inside.

"Matt?" Thomas whispered loud enough so the whisper would bounce off of the ceramic tiles, making his voice heard throughout the room. But there was no answer.

Thomas walked all the way in and bent over to see if any legs hung down from the stalls, but he saw no legs. He then walked over to each stall, opening the metal doors slowly. The last thing Thomas wanted was to peep on a stall in use and be titled a *gazer*.

The first stall—nothing; the second stall—also nothing; the third was the same, all the way to the sixth stall. They were all empty. This was now a great mystery. No one left the hall at night unless he had an order to appear somewhere the next day, and Matt did not have any order as far as Thomas knew.

This became a dilemma. If Thomas told the guards that Matt was gone while Matt was just hiding, Thomas would be labeled a *rat*, and no one wants that title. If you are labeled a rat, you might as well be dead; no one will speak to a rat. However, if Matt was hurt, Thomas could not forgive himself if he did not help find him. Thomas felt inadequate to make a decision and began to panic.

"I need some help or a guide," Thomas said between his teeth. "Yeah, a guide, just like Sal. He was always wise when trouble came."

Thomas realized that if God had been communicating to him through his dream, then God made Sal part of that dream to teach Thomas. Why couldn't Thomas be wise like Sal in this moment? Instead of stressing about his choices, Thomas focused on his surroundings to see if anything could help him solve Matt's disappearance. Nothing in the bathroom was out of place.

Thomas returned to the hallway and saw that the guard still

slept. His first instinct was to pass the guard as fast as possible, but as he scurried by, he noticed something different about the guard. The security card the guard wore around his neck was missing. The guard still wore the lanyard the card attached to, indicating the guard had the card at one time. But the card was missing.

Thomas crept further down the hall and observed that the door to the main room had not shut completely. Every time a guard shuts a secure door, he always checks it to make sure it's shut completely. This indicated to Thomas that it wasn't a guard who had last gone through the door. *Matt must have tried to escape,* Thomas thought, *but why? Matt is the calmest boy in prison.*

Thomas realized the reason wasn't presently important and continued investigating. He opened the door to the main room, but before releasing it, he grabbed a chair and propped it in the doorway so it would not close behind him. Next he looked for signs of Matt's escape in the main room, but it was dark and hard to see. Thomas checked the two main doors, but they were secure. Thomas became angry when he couldn't quickly find another clue but calmed himself and focused.

"The rear door," Thomas mumbled out loud. *Yes,* he thought. *The door I came in when I was first brought here.* Nobody had been brought through that door since Thomas came. He tiptoed like a cat toward the rear door, trying not to make noise. He came to the rear double doors and lightly pushed against the right one; it was secure. Thomas knew that if the left door did not move, his investigation would be over. He would have to return to his room and tell the guard about Matt. He took a deep breath and then pressed the left door; it felt secure. Thomas sighed and then put his arm on the left door, fearing he would be forced to tell the guard about Matt. He sunk his head into his arm. The door budged.

"Whoa, this is great," Thomas said with a new spirit. But that spirit did not last, for as he opened the door, he said, "Blood?"

Thomas saw a pool of blood on the concrete just barely visible under the pale yellow security light. The blood still trickled down the barbed-wire fence. He gazed at the small hole though the razor-wire fence with blood on the tips of the sharp edges.

"Matt," called Thomas in a forceful whisper, but there was no answer. The decision was clear; he had to tell the guard. Thomas returned through the double doors and ran across the main room and back into the hallway to wake the sleeping guard. Thomas shook the guard's shoulder. "Hey, sir. Help, help," he said.

"What the … hey!" The guard woke thinking Thomas was trying to attack him, so he grabbed Thomas by the arm, stood up, and took Thomas to the ground facedown. "What's wrong with you, kid?" the guard shouted. "You just itching for a red shirt?"

"No, no sir," Thomas mumbled with his lips to the ground. "My roommate is gone, and there's blood on the ground outside."

"How do you know what's outside? Were you with him?" the guard grunted. "You're just a chicken who was with him, and you got scared and decided to rat." The guard put plastic flex cuffs on Thomas's hands.

"Sir, no! I wasn't with him. I woke up and he was gone and …" Thomas tried to explain, but the guard didn't listen.

"G20," the guard said into his radio. "I have a breach in sector A. Two escapees—I have one detained. Initiate a perimeter for the other." The guard looked at Thomas. "Who was your partner?" he yelled.

By this time the other boys had heard the commotion and come to the doors of their cells. The guard then jumped up and hit a button that locked all the cell doors, keeping the boys inside. More guards flooded the hallway. The guard brought Thomas back to his bedroom and placed him on the chair.

"So you thought you were going to escape, huh?" the guard said, shaking his head up and down.

"No, I didn't think that. I wasn't trying to escape," Thomas protested. "Look, sir, I don't want trouble with you or anyone, but think about it: if I were trying to escape, why would I come and wake you up?"

"Because," the guard returned, "you got scared and came back to rat so you wouldn't go down."

"Please sir, I'm scared for my friend. There was a puddle of blood, and he didn't answer when I called to him." The guard put up a wall, blocking Thomas's requests. He sat down on Matt's abandoned bunk.

"Huh, your friend made his bunk before he left," the guard said. "What an odd kid. Wait, what's this?" The guard grabbed a piece of paper tucked halfway under Matt's pillow. "It says 'To Thomas,'" the guard read. "Is that you?" the guard said, looking at Thomas. Thomas nodded.

The guard opened the paper and read, "Thomas, when you read this letter, it means that I have left. I have another sentencing trial coming, and they might put me in adult prison. I'm not ready for that. I couldn't accept that I had to be here for what I did. Like I said, those three seconds will haunt me forever. I wanted you to know that I thought you were different from all the other kids here, and I was proud to share a room with you. I need to go find that lifeline we talked about. I need to show that I'm not a criminal, just a coward who acted too late. Keep it real, Thomas. Matt."

The guard looked up silently at Thomas.

"See, sir, I was not with him. Please, we need to find out if he is okay," Thomas pleaded. Just then another guard entered.

"Is this the other escapee?" he asked, looking at the other guard and pointing at Thomas.

The first guard hesitated. "No, this is his roommate."

"I thought you said you had two escapees."

"I was wrong; this one here was trying to tell me about the other one leaving," the first guard said.

"Ah, a rat huh?"

"No, he's no rat. He's a good kid looking out for his buddy," the first guard said, looking Thomas in the eyes. "He thought his buddy was hurt."

"That's why I'm here. They can't find the other kid, but there's so much blood they don't think he got far. The bosses want this guy to come and try to call his friend to see if he will respond to his voice."

Both guards then escorted Thomas outside. "Here," said the first guard. "Let me cut those things off of you," he said, grabbing the plastic flex cuffs on Thomas's wrists.

"Thanks," Thomas said as he looked up at the guard.

They walked out to the rear doors where Thomas had seen the pool of blood under the razor wire. This time, the whole yard was bright with floodlights, and Thomas saw how much blood was pooled on both sides of the razor-wire fence. The jagged, sharp hole in the fence was two feet high by one foot long, which would have made it difficult for Matt's large body to have fit through. This explained all the blood. Each tip of the jagged fence must have torn Matt's flesh like an eagle's talons as he pulled his body through the hole. The floodlights exposed the whole yard, making the Olympic-sized pool visible. It looked like a giant, greenish-brown Jell-O mold. The trickle of water beneath the diving board frothed up dirty bubbles which threw dirty, viscous water splats onto the concrete, becoming dry, solid scum.

"Bring him over here," a deep, gruff voice boomed. It came from the night warden, who was a very fat man. "What's your name, son?"

"I'm Thomas, sir."

"Okay, Thomas. We need you to call out to your friend. Let him know that you are here and that nobody here wants to hurt him. We just want him to be safe."

"Why would you want me to say that?" Thomas asked, feeling confused.

"Because he'll listen to you. It will give him that psychological edge he needs to motivate himself to come out. Now go ahead. Do it; I don't think he has much time."

Thomas cleared his throat, "Matt! Matt, it's me, Thomas! I'm here. I guess you know that because you can hear me." The guards and the warden looked at each other and then down at Thomas. Thomas felt nervous.

"It's here ... I mean, I'm here, and I'm okay. I mean it's okay, Matt. The guards just want to help!" There was no response. Thomas could hear the small trickle in the background. "Matt!" He called again, "I've got your lifeline! I know what it is."

Thomas paused, but there was no reply. Again he heard the small trickle and turned his head in the direction of the pool. He saw the scum patches on the concrete next to the spout. But as he stared harder, he saw the patches were making a trail. Thomas followed the trail and saw it led back to the pool of blood by the razor fence.

Thomas walked over to the trail and saw that it was not scum but a path of blood.

"He's in the pool," shouted Thomas. Everyone rushed to the pool, hoping to see Matt, but the thick, black water prevented any view. Some of the guards grabbed poles and poked though the scum to feel him. The efforts to find Matt were not working. The pool was too big to check with poles; they needed to get to the middle of the pool. *But how?* thought Thomas to himself. Thomas surveyed the yard for anything that could help.

"That's it," Thomas said as he saw a small raft the boys made when they used to use the pool. He rushed over, grabbed the raft and a pole, and threw them into the large, scummy pool.

"Son, don't," cried the night warden. "We'll have to rescue you also."

"It's fine," shouted Thomas. "I know what I'm doing."

Thomas stepped onto the raft and put the pole into the water, pushing himself off the side and into the middle of the pool. At first Thomas waded through the pool, using his pole to find any sign of Matt, but the pool was too large and there was only one raft. Feeling inadequate, Thomas began to panic. He stared down at the scummy pool and near tears, said, "Matt, I've got the lifeline. Matt, please come up. I've got it. It's the rope."

The rope, Thomas thought to himself. He remembered what the guard said about the ropes built to drain the pool. He stared at the black film on top of the water, which seemed to eat the light from the flood lamps. The pool was not only gross but also scary—evil. Thomas realized that Matt could no longer help himself. Thomas would need to leave the comforts of the raft on the surface to find the rope below and save Matt.

"What happened, kid?" yelled the night warden. "Why did you stop?"

"The ropes," Thomas yelled back. "The ropes at the bottom of the pool. Will they still drain the pool?"

"There's no way to know, kid. That's foolish, though. You'll be in worse shape than your friend if you go down there."

"I've got to try; there's no more time." Thomas jumped into the black, scummy pool. It felt like he was swimming in thick, pulpy orange juice. It felt like minutes before he reached the bottom. Thomas's lungs began to burn, and he feared he would not have enough air and energy to pull the rope if he found it. Thomas held his arms in front of him, hoping to feel the rope—but there was nothing. He felt the burning in his lungs, as if he had swallowed hot sauce.

There was not much more he could do; Thomas held his arms out at his sides to begin the swim back up. As he extended his arm, he felt something slimy on his left side. He reached for it; it was the rope. Thomas grabbed the rope and put it between his legs as he put his feet on the bottom of the pool. He pulled the rope as hard as he could and then swam back to the surface before his lungs gave out. Thomas broke the surface of the water, flinging scum particles over the guards near the edge. "Did it work?" Thomas gasped, as he grabbed the edge of the pool.

"There's no light," the night warden said. "That red light over there is supposed to come on if the rope were ever pulled." A guard walked over to the lightless bulb and gave it a solid punch.

"The light!" Thomas shouted as everybody stared at the glowing red light, which now pulsated on and off. Then, just as Thomas pulled himself out of the pool, a giant gurgle erupted from the pool.

"The water is going down," shouted the warden. "Kid, you did it!"

Everybody stared at the surface waiting to see any sign of Matt's body. For two minutes all were silent as they watched the water slowly drain.

"Over here," shouted a guard, pointing to a scum-covered mass. Immediately the guards jumped into the knee-high shallow muck water and picked up the still lump that was Matt's body. Paramedics flung him onto a hospital gurney and checked for signs of life.

"You're going too, kid," the night warden said to Thomas as paramedics put him on a second gurney. "You're going need medical help after going in that cesspool."

"But Matt—what about him? Is he going to live?" Thomas asked, coming to tears.

"I don't know, son, but if he does, it's because you had the faith that that rope would still be there."

CHAPTER 20

THE CALLING

THOMAS RETURNED TO the Juvenile Department of Corrections after being released from the hospital, where he was treated for a multitude of toxins he had ingested in the swimming pool. For his heroic actions, Thomas received a green shirt; however, he also received another year in prison for violating federal swimming pool drainage laws. As he walked into his cell, he noticed Matt's empty bunk. No one had told Thomas if Matt lived or died, causing Thomas to drown in thoughts of self-inflicted guilt. If Matt was alive, Thomas wondered if he had influenced Matt negatively, causing Matt to leave; but if Matt was dead, then Thomas felt he had not alerted the guards quickly enough to have saved Matt's life. Either way, Thomas felt guilty and prayed that God would pull him out of the whirlpool of guilty thought.

When he wasn't feeling guilty about Matt, Thomas searched for evidence of his own changed life. Thomas figured that if his river dream helped him find Matt, then more situations existed for Thomas to assist others. During the morning roll call, Thomas noticed a kid who had received a red shirt for flinging his thick mashed potatoes at a guard. After the roll call broke up, Thomas approached the new red shirt.

"Hey man, my name is Thomas," he said looking at the red shirt's face.

"Yup, I know," said the red shirt kid, staring at wall in front of him and not at Thomas. "You're the big hero around here now Mr. Green Shirt Savior."

"I don't know about that," Thomas said, giving a nervous laugh. "I just figured maybe I could help out a little."

"What do you mean help?" said the red shirt as he turned toward Thomas, looking offended. "You mean help me like your old red-shirted roommate who you 'helped' and now is probably dead?"

"No, look," said Thomas, reaching out his opened-palmed hand toward the kid, "I just thought we could talk."

"Talk. You think we can talk?" the kid said to Thomas, scanning his face for sarcasm. "And what are we going to talk about there, green-shirted Thomas?"

Thomas realized he only knew about the river. He figured that if the dream was a communication from God, then it would have the ability to make its meaning known to all who would hear it. He went for it. "I just wanted to say that life is like a river."

"What?" yelled the red-shirt kid, convinced Thomas was playing a joke on him. "Dude, you're an idiot!" he yelled as he got up and walked away.

Thomas didn't move. He felt the same frustration someone feels when his car does not start or when a light in the room goes out. The river dream was supposed to work with a simple flick of the tongue. That night Thomas fell asleep, frustrated at the dream once again. Thomas felt it should have worked, but why had it not?

At times, a group from a religious college visited the boys' prison. They wore tan cloth pants that hugged their tucked-in polo shirts.

Every time one of them addressed a kid in the prison, he called the kid buddy or partner; this had the same plastic effect as a politician calling someone he had never met "my friend." The college students would toss a football or kick the soccer ball around. They tried to play basketball, but their shiny dress shoes kept slipping on the concrete.

Sometimes a kid pretended to be interested in what one of the college students said, but later the college student would notice his wallet was missing. Other kids, however, seemed to like the attention the students gave them. The students and the boys would exchange fist bumps. Sometimes you could see a student putting his arm around a kid who was wiping away a tear from his own eye; this only lasted until the boy thought someone was watching, at which time he shrugged off the student's arm. To many boys, the college students became their only positive role models. The guards had to be there—it was their job—but the students chose to come on their own free time. It was their passion. As goofy and inorganic as the college students appeared on the outside, they gave the boys genuine personal interaction.

After an attempt at sports, the students would gather the boys together for a religious message. Thomas attended when he could, but he sat toward the rear. Wearing a green shirt at the religious meetings meant you were a spy, a rat. Thomas listened to the students challenge the boys to reach for high goals and strive for excellence in their minds, souls, and bodies. Thomas had heard talk like this when he attended church with his mother. He remembered how annoying and irrelevant the message sounded back then, like a bad song on a radio over which he had no control. This time, however, Thomas agreed with what he heard. He understood he had to improve himself—that he had to develop his own relationship with God by believing that God really wanted to communicate with him.

Thomas now enjoyed the message the same way an adult enjoys the vegetables he hated as a child. But something was wrong. A mental gap separated the students from the prisoners.

One student who was wearing a crisply pressed polo shirt and pleated pants once said in a speech, "You need to forgive you enemies. I remember a time when my neighbor and friend, John, took my brand new bike I got for Christmas—"

"Go John!" shouted one of the boys.

"No, no," said the student, pumping his open hands up and down to cool down the outburst. "It was a very sad time for me. At first I was angry at John, and I wanted to punch him in the nose."

"That's right!" shouted another boy.

"No. That would have been wrong," the student continued, attempting authority. "I prayed about the matter, and I knew I had to forgive him. It was very hard for me, but eventually I went to John's house and told him I forgave him. Then he and I both took my bike and got ice cream."

"So you're saying," began a boy in the crowd, "that I need to go get ice cream with the thug who shot my pop for his crack rock?" The crowd began to hoot like monkeys.

The student's eyes widened, and his mouth opened. "I'm … I'm sorry," the student stammered, trying to gain control of the crowd. "I don't know how something like that would feel. But I know that Jesus forgives us of our sin if we ask him, and we need to forgive others as well. Jesus is the answer."

"What does he answer?" shouted a boy who stood up and shook his hands at the student. "How does he answer my mama sending me to live with my grandma because she wants to live with her boyfriend who hates kids?" The other kids stood up, shouting loudly and causing the guards to come and maintain order.

Jesus is the answer, Thomas thought, but he understood that the college students knew the answer without understanding the problem. Thomas saw the gap separating the groups as if he were watching the sun rise over the Grand Canyon. The boys well understood the problem, but they could not see how to reach the answer. The college students told the boys to look at the answers, just like Mr. Modstiff told Thomas to look at answers in the back of the math book without showing him how to do the work. Thomas realized the red-shirt kid had rejected him because he tried to give the red shirt kid the answer without acknowledging the problem; the answer has no place without a problem.

Thomas walked away from the group, floating along like a lonely cloud. He wandered into his room and lay down on his bunk.

"I get it now," Thomas said, almost praying out loud. "My time on the Rio Vida was no dream: It was a calling." Thomas felt goose bumps, just like someone listening to his favorite song after not hearing it for a long time. Thomas then popped off his bunk and sought the kid in the red shirt.

"What do you want?" said the kid as he saw Thomas approaching.

"I want you to listen," said Thomas with authority. The kid looked at Thomas, giving him permission to continue. "You either had a bad father or no father at all. Right?"

"Right," the red shirt kid acknowledged, slightly puzzled. "But how do you know that?"

"That one's easy," Thomas said. "Every kid here has that same situation. There might be one kid that had a good dad and still managed to screw himself up enough to earn a place here, but I'll take my chances you're not him." The red shirt kid nodded and gave a look that begged Thomas to continue. "I'm trying to tell you that you were put on the path of your life by people who cared more about themselves than about you, and that part is not your fault."

"My dad left me and my mom when I was eight," the kid confessed. "He left for some other woman. He said he would come back for me, but he had a baby with his new lady. She did not want me around. She said I might be a bad influence on their baby because I lived with my mom. My mom, on the other hand, thought I looked too much like my father and treated me bad because she saw everything she hated about him in me."

"Yes, that's what I mean," began Thomas. "That part was not your fault. But listen to me for a second." Thomas explained how life flows like a river and how we can't control time, but we can control what we do with the time. He then talked about having faith and how each person had to find faith by leaving the comfort of the raft of his life.

"I get it," said the red-shirted kid, "but what has that got to do with all of us having crappy fathers?"

"It means that none of us have any excuse to screw up our lives just because our fathers sucked. God will be a father to you if you let him."

Just then, the guard came in to gather all the boys together for science class. The college students had left, and mandatory school began.

"Hello, boys," said an older, chubby man with white hair and a scruffy beard. Thomas stared at him for a while. He reminded him of someone he had met before. "My name is Professor Charles Boomington."

Could it be, thought Thomas. *Was it … Boom?* Thomas sat back in shock, not wanting to sound ridiculous to the professor or the other boys. What if it wasn't him?

"I teach natural science at the university," the professor continued. "Today I'd like to begin on a basic science lesson discussing the difference between fact and theory. Facts are things I can prove to you by demonstration, and if I repeat the demonstration, we will see the same result every time. A theory is something I cannot prove to you with demonstration. It is something I believe to be true based on other facts that I can prove."

He walked around the room as he talked, speaking with a soothing voice, as if he were a grandfather telling a story by the fire. As Thomas stared at him, he noticed the professor had burly brown rope around his waist acting as a belt.

"Professor," Thomas said as he raised his hand.

"Yes, son, what is it?"

"I noticed your belt." The other boys chuckled, not understanding what it was that Thomas was really asking. "What does it represent, a fact or a theory?"

Thomas and the professor exchanged a stare lasting so long that the other boys stopped chuckling and began thinking Thomas would be in trouble for his question. Thomas felt uneasy, as if the professor were looking directly, deeply into his soul. Finally the professor slowly released a thin, knowing smile, just like a long-awaited sunrise on a cold morning.

"This, son, is evidence of a theory I know to be a fact but will never be able to prove it to anyone by demonstration. It is something I at one time hated, but I have come to value its preciousness."

The statement made Thomas smile, and as Thomas's smile grew, the professor matched it with his own. Soon the other boys realized that Thomas and the professor shared an understanding of the rope that was hidden from the rest. The professor finished his lesson, and Thomas approached the front of the class to speak with him; but by the time he reached the front of the class, the professor had left. Professor Charles Boomington never taught at the boys' prison again.

CHAPTER 21

VICTORY

A FEW MONTHS later, Thomas exchanged his green department of corrections shirt and for a green army uniform. Months earlier the army recruiter had come to the boys' prison, announcing a program that allowed imprisoned juveniles close to the age of eighteen to join the army to shorten their sentences. Thomas just completed his high school program and qualified for army enlistment. Thomas felt he had no skills to sustain himself outside of prison; therefore, the promised twenty thousand dollars for enlistment made Thomas feel like he made a wise choice.

The boys at the prison felt sad to see Thomas leave. Lately Thomas became known as "Preacher Tom" because of his efforts to tell the boys that God wanted to be their father. Some boys rejected Thomas, but most knew Thomas sincerely cared about them—that he wasn't just repeating things he heard at a church service. They felt Thomas spoke as if he had somehow seen God.

Before he left, Ken came to wish Thomas good-bye, and he brought Gracie, who was now seven years old.

"Gracie, honey, do you remember me?" Thomas asked as he knelt down in the visitor's center, reaching toward the little girl holding Ken's hand. She had grown twice her size since Thomas had last seen her.

"Is that my brother?" she asked in a voice far from the lispy talk from the three-year-old Thomas last heard.

"Yes, sweetheart," Ken said softly. "I think he would really like a hug."

"Okay!" she shouted and ran to Thomas, grabbing him by the neck and squeezing almost to the point of suffocation. "My daddy, mommy, and I pray for you every night."

Thomas squeezed her back. Ken had told Thomas earlier that Gracie had no memory of Thomas from before, but she knew Thomas from the stories Ken told her about him. Thomas felt she lived up to her name once again, gracefully giving Thomas love and relieving him of the guilt of not being able to care for her like a big brother should. He knew she was loved by a good family that was led by a good man. This gave Thomas peace.

"I'm proud of you, Thomas," Ken said. "This will be a good chance for you to lead other soldiers like you led the other prisoners."

"How's Abby?" Thomas asked quickly, knowing the answer would not be pleasing.

"She got married a few months ago to some guy she met at college," Ken said nonchalantly, not understanding how Thomas felt about her. "His father was a pastor of a church in the Midwest. He got a degree in finance and began working for some religious book company."

"That's great," Thomas said with a trumped-up smile, hiding his fractured hart.

"Graves, let's move, the bus is leaving," shouted a guard to Thomas.

"Thank you, Ken," Thomas said as he held out his hand to deliver a firm handshake.

"No, thank you, Thomas," Ken said as he grabbed Thomas's arm and pulled him into a big hug. "You have taught me so much about God, life, and love. Because of you, I now see how personal and loving God is to me and to all of us. I will pray for you every day."

Thomas conquered boot camp without a problem. He never became an official leader in his class, but the other recruits would say that Thomas inspired them with his belief that God had placed them all together on purpose. He left boot camp to fight in Afghanistan, where he fought bravely, but those who have never fought for their lives would never understand these stories. Therefore, Thomas never spoke much about them. Thomas's metaphor of life as a river and a rope as saving faith comforted many soldiers who had nothing else to carry them through the fog of war.

After returning home, Thomas collected his signing bonus for twenty thousand dollars. At age twenty-two this seemed like lots of money in the same way a teenager seems to be a full-grown adult to a child. Thomas watched his army buddies spend their money on valueless parties and clueless women. Others invested their money in education, but reading books and writing reports failed to compare with the education they had received from war. Thomas decided to invest in people; he would start a business to help people understand their own need for the rope and to find the answer by working through the problem of their lives.

"I would like to know about the property at 1524 Main Street, please," said Thomas to the clerk at city hall.

"The old Stainkins's gas station?" asked the clerk, scratching his head. "Why would you want anything to do with that?"

"Who would I talk to about getting that property?" Thomas asked.

"Well," began the clerk, "one would just need to pay the back taxes on the property."

"How do I find out how much money that would be?"

"Let me see if we have the records on that," said the clerk as he went to the back room. As Thomas waited, he looked around the city hall and saw the pictures of all the police officers and firefighters who had died protecting his small city. He thought about other small towns and cities across the country and how many officers must have died protecting them. He remembered his army buddies and how many had died protecting the country. He realized that few understood how much sacrifice and blood it cost to maintain a small town's peace, let alone a whole country, and then how much blood for all mankind.

"That's ten thousand, five hundred and forty dollars even," said the clerk, bringing Thomas out of his trance.

"What? I'm sorry," Thomas said, refocusing.

"The amount for the property you asked about," the clerk said slowly.

"Yes, who do I pay that to?" asked Thomas.

"Well, that would be here," said the clerk. "But why would you care about such a dump?"

"Because I need to give hope to someone who lost it long ago."

After Thomas paid the back taxes, he drove to the old station and opened the chain-link fence with a key the city had given him. He looked at the old building, staring at the rounded, white plaster art deco corners. He walked in and saw that Johnny Cash's "A Boy Named Sue" was the last record played on the broken down jukebox.

"Let's try this again, Jangk," Thomas said softly.

Over the next few months, construction crews worked on the building under the orders that they were to make the building as close to the original design as possible, with a few modifications. Thomas had the pleasure of opening the Rio Vida Café and the

Santa Fe Bookstore. Thomas felt people craved food and knowledge and this was the best way to fuse the cravings together. Many church and social groups used Thomas's business for meetings; it became the best place to pitch a new idea and to defend old ones.

Thomas enjoyed the customers; he challenged them to leave the comfort of their lives and search for the rope of faith he knew would be waiting for them. Gracie helped wash dishes and clean tables on the weekends. She gave customers the delightful smile her mother would have given had she not been trampled by life's weight.

One day as Thomas worked the counter, he heard a voice he had not heard in a long time.

"Tommy," said the woman's voice softly. Thomas felt a warm feeling travel from his head to his feet. He knew the voice well.

With his back facing, the woman, he said, "I've had many storms on my river, but I'm not sure I'm ready to face this one."

"This isn't your storm, Tommy, it's mine," she said.

Thomas turned and wrapped his eyes around the only woman to ever possess his heart. Abby had the same long brown hair, only fuller and deeper. Her eyes glowed like candles, bringing light to a dark room. Her face looked like a woman's face, slightly older than he remembered but in a way that showed knowledge and not age. He felt love for her instantly—love, not lust. He wanted to embrace her and not disgrace her. But that could not happen; another man had pledged to be one flesh with her, and nothing but the rope itself was more sacred. As Thomas looked down, he saw a delightful little girl who looked just like Abby holding her hand. He also noticed Abby's stomach protruding from her body.

"Thomas, this is Victory. She's three almost four," Abby said, looking into Thomas's eyes, "She won't be a storm on your river. I hope I will not be a storm either."

"Where is your husband?" Thomas asked, disciplining his emotion.

"We're divorced. He left me," she said, lowering her head.

"How is that possible?" Thomas asked in disbelief, as if someone had told him a man had declined a billion dollars.

"He left the first time someone offered him something he felt was more exciting. Let's just say for now that he never attached himself to the rope beneath the river."

Thomas looked at her as if she spoke an ancient word that only Thomas understood. "You mean …"

"Yes. My father told me all about your dream, your vision. I would love to hear more. I would love to be a part of it somehow," she stated with her eyes down, as if she felt ashamed for not understanding the vision before.

"I can't think of anything I would like better. When can we talk?" he asked, lifting her chin lightly, resisting the urge to jump over the counter and pick her up in his arms. Thomas felt God himself had brought this moment to pass.

"Victory here likes to race her bike. You know, like on a BMX track, on dirt. It's funny; her father always thought she needed to be more lady-like. But every time we would pass the race track, she would shout, 'I race, Mommy, I race.' I finally took her one weekend, and she got third place and a trophy. She raced five boys and got a third place."

"Did her father ever go with her?" asked Thomas.

"He never had time … for that anyway," Abby said, dropping her head again, placing her eyes to the ground.

Thomas looked down at her with glazed eyes, mesmerized by the moment and impressed with Abby's daughter. Victory reached up to Thomas and held out her arms; Thomas picked her up and held her. "You come watch me," she said in a tiny voice.

"Victory," Thomas said as he picked her up. "God did answer my prayer. God gave me Victory." Thomas knew full well that God had taken care of him, but now he realized it was more than care; it was preparation, grooming so Thomas could now give others the gift of fatherhood God had given him.

"Ouch," yelped Thomas as ran his hand through Victory's hair. "Why do you have fishhooks in your hair?"

"I don't know how that got there," Abby said as she plucked it out of her daughter's hair.

"Maybe someone else asked for them," Thomas said, shaking his poked finger.

After asking Ken for his blessing, Thomas married Abby three months later—just in time for the new baby, which Abby insisted they name Thomas Jr. Thomas adopted Victory and Thomas Jr. When asked by the judge why he would make a good father, Thomas stated "God wants me to be a father to the fatherless, just like he has been to me." He then looked at Abby. "And I could not think of a better woman in the world to raise these wonderful kids with."

Thomas and Abby had a loving and realistic marriage. They loved, they fought, they made up, and they loved again, over and over. No child in the world received as much time with his or her father as Victory and Thomas Jr. When he was not at the café and bookstore, Thomas was with Victory at the BMX race track helping her become a competitive racer. As soon as Thomas Jr. was old enough, he too raced with Victory. Thomas and Abby had another child they named Mathew. As soon as Mathew could waddle, the whole family worked together in the café and bookstore. The business became one of the most successful places in the county. Church groups, college students, and politicians sharpened their ideas and clarified their visions at the Santa Fe Book Store. Sojourners came seeking answers and left knowing the answer could not merely be looked up in the back of the book.

One day an old man walked into the store in a white, button-up, collared shirt tucked into khaki pants. He had an old fedora on his head that shadowed his face. Thomas had his back turned to the old man as he approached the counter.

"You the new owner?" said the old man in a gruff voice that sounded like it had survived years of smoking.

"Yes, yes sir I am," Thomas said with his back still turned, stocking the shelves. "I'll be right with you."

"Oh, no need. Keep working. I'm not looking for any books. I just wanted to say this place looks great and that the old owner would be pleased with what you did with the place. I think he would want you to know that you helped him more that you can possibly comprehend." The old man's words crawled into Thomas's skin, producing goose bumps; he turned around to speak to the man.

"Did you know the previous owner?" Thomas asked an empty bookstore. Thomas smelled the faint odor of something burnt; on the counter he saw a charred piece of rope still smoldering. He stared at it and noticed divots, as if someone had clutched it tightly for a long time. As he reached to pick it up, the front door flung open.

"Are you Thomas Graves?" asked a frantic, middle-aged Hispanic lady.

"Yes, are you all right? Can I help you?"

"I pray that you can," she said as she pulled out a chair and sat down. "You never met me, but I am the mother of Mathew Gonzales."

"Matt!" shouted Thomas. "They never told me what happened to him after that night at the prison pool." Thomas had always feared Matt had died.

"I need you to talk to Mathew for me now," she said, placing her hand on her head.

"He's alive!" shouted Thomas. "How come nobody told me he lived?"

"Yes, he is alive, in a way. You never heard anything else because his condition was so serious that they had to move him to a level-one hospital out of state. You see, he has been in a coma ever since that night."

"All these years?" Thomas asked.

"Yes, all these years. The doctors have always told me that he is dead inside and that I should not tease myself by keeping him on the machines. But I just know he is alive inside. The other night I was praying to God that he would give me some hope or a sign so I might show the doctors I am right. Then they can tell my insurance that it is necessary to keep Mathew on those machines. You see, they want to take him off. They say he is an unnecessary expense. So I prayed, and the next day Mathew mumbled something over and over. At first I could not understand, but soon I heard him to say, 'Tell Thomas Graves … I can't find Sal.'"

"Matt's on the river," Thomas said softly to himself.

"Where?" questioned Mat's mother, frustrated.

"He's safe, ma'am," Thomas said with a smooth, content smile. "He is dealing with his father."

"His father!" she cried violently. "He never knew his father, and those men in his life were horrible replacements." She put her head in her arms and mumbled, "His whole life he has been fatherless."

"Exactly," Thomas said as he placed his hand on her back to comfort her. "He will now see that God is the father of the fatherless."